Collision

Kate L. Mary

Collision

:

~DEDICATION~

For the nerd of my dreams, Jeremy, who has always been there to support and believe in me.

Collision

CONTENTS

Collision

ACKNOWLEDGMENTS

When I started writing I had no idea what a difficult field I was trying to break into. Honestly, if it wasn't for all the amazing support I've gotten from the friends who have read my books, I don't know if I would have made it. So, I have to extend a very huge thank you to all my friends and guinea pigs, who read my books in various stages, ranging from crappy to fantastic. Without their enthusiasm I'm not sure I could have kept going. A very special thanks goes out to Erin Rose, my best friend who was the first reader on almost all my projects. My other first readers and cheerleaders include: Sarah McVay, Tammy Moore-Brewer, Marly Pederson, Cherith Peters, Casey Star, Lyden Pelbath, Darcy Ceccoli, Russ James, Rebekah Caillouet, Amy Mary, Kim Roth, Colette Ricketts and Diana Gardin.

A huge thanks to my number one critique partner and beta reader, Lisa Terry. Her direction and tough-love helped shape my writing and bring out the best, and I know for a fact I couldn't have done with without her.

Thank you to Emily Teng, who spent hours editing this book when it was still in the hands of my previous publisher, and Jimmy Gibbs for the great cover art.

I also want to thank my parents for raising me to be such a confident person. In a field where you hear no so much more than yes, it's difficult to maintain a positive attitude. If I hadn't been raised to believe in myself the way I have, I don't know that I would have been able to keep going.

To Jeremy, my amazingly supportive husband who has watched our four kids for hours on end so I could edit and revise, and write something new that might never get published. There is nothing more amazing than having a partner who is openly supportive of you.

A huge thank you to my kids, who have endured hours of me staring at a computer screen. Carter, Christa, Corinne and Chase, I love you and hope that one day your dreams will come true too, no matter what they are.

Collision

CHAPTER ONE

When I open my eyes, the world is a blur of noise and lights that spins around me like a tornado. Red, blue. Red, blue. White. The white makes my head pound. The lights swirl until my head threatens to split in half, and I have to squint against the pounding glow of colors. I'm dizzy with pain, but even more agonizing is the noise. Muffled voices and the crunch of metal and glass. It bears down, spiraling around me and pressing me into a tight ball until I can't breathe. Suffocating me.

My chest is tight, as if something is sitting on me. My lungs are on fire, screaming for relief. I gasp, but only manage to get a teaspoonful of air, and my hands fly to my torso. Something *is* there. Something hard and immovable. My breath comes out in short gasps as I try to pull it away, but it doesn't budge. The textured surface is familiar, but the pain in my lungs and the noise in my ears and the lights blinding me make it impossible to focus.

I *need* to focus.

I grip the surface harder. What's the last thing I can remember? Where am I? A memory flashes through my mind. Darkness cloaked in a thick blanket of white. Snow.

I was driving in the snow. Then the world spun out of control. Then pain. So much pain. It all comes flooding back, and my lungs tighten even more. I must have had an accident, and now I'm trapped. I'm going to die.

My world spins a little more, and the white lights brighten. Even with my eyes closed they penetrate my eyelids. My hands are still gripping the steering wheel—*that's* what's pressing against me—and my arms shake. The weight on my chest threatens to crush me. I push and squirm and gasp, but the pressure doesn't subside, and a slow agonizing fire burns in my chest.

Something crunches near my face and I want to scream, but I don't have enough air. All I manage is a small whimper, like a sick little dog. Something taps against the window, and it takes me a second to focus my eyes. The windshield has splintered into a thousand tiny cracks. I squint at the glass, and my eyes sting. I can just make out a person on the other side.

"Help."

The scratchy sound that comes out of my mouth isn't a word. My eyes sting even more, but when the sobs try to escape I want to scream. My body shakes, pressing me against the steering wheel. Splinters of pain radiate through every inch of my torso.

The person taps again and leans closer, yelling at me through the cracks. His voice is so deep it almost drowns out all the other noise. "Close your eyes and turn your face away."

I react without thinking and squeeze my eyes shut. The world around me shatters, and crinkles, like yards of bubble wrap being balled up and tossed aside. Only louder and more terrifying. I can't keep my eyes closed, and when I open them the man is so close I can feel his hot breath on my face.

"Help." This time it sounds more like a word, but it's still barely a whisper. There's no way he heard it, but he nods like he understands.

"Hang on!" he yells, and his hand covers mine, still wrapped around the steering wheel.

He turns to shout over his shoulder, and other people come toward me. They're all dressed alike in suits the color of spicy mustard. They swim around me, and my heart thumps to the beat of a strange metallic drum. No, not a drum. The whirling sound of a motor.

The guy holding my hand leans forward. "We have to use the Jaws of Life."

My brain feels fuzzy, like I just woke up or I've been drinking, and the words don't make sense at first. A man comes forward holding a piece of machinery. They're going to cut me out. Somehow it's more terrifying than not being able to breathe. Thankfully, the guy still has my hand. I don't want to be alone.

I shut my eyes, but open them back up when his hand moves off mine. He's still there, and he yells something to me about protection. All I can think about is condoms, but that doesn't make sense. Am I hallucinating?

Someone hands him a blanket, and he lays it across my body. He leans in closer to bring it up to my face. "I'll be right here the whole time!"

The blanket is heavy and scratchy, and it's even more difficult to breathe with it pressed against my face. But a hand wraps around mine, and it helps hold off the panic when the crunch of metal and glass rips through the car. My lungs throb. Tears fall down my cheeks, but I can't even get enough air to really cry.

When the heaviness falls away from my chest and I finally get a big mouthful of air, the pain is almost too much. An ache spreads across my body from the inside out. But I can't stop. I can't keep my lungs from gasping for air, sucking it in like a man on death row getting his last glimpse of the sun. It sends a pleasant ache through my body.

The blanket is pulled away, and I'm met by the swirl of snow against the dark, night sky. Cool air surrounds me, and the world becomes a blur again. Red, blue. White. Red, blue. More shouting, more metal. This time it's louder and brighter because the roof of my car has been peeled away. The same guy is in front of me. He squeezes my hand once before letting it go, but he doesn't move. More people join him and suddenly half a dozen faces fight for my attention.

"We need to put this on you," a woman says. Unlike the others, her shirt is dark blue. She wraps a stiff collar around my neck. It's almost as constricting as the pain in my lungs, and now I feel like someone is sitting on my chest with their fingers wrapped around my throat.

I reach up to pull at it, but the same man tugs my hand away. "You need it." The gentle tone breaks through my confusion and helps ease the terror.

Everyone is talking at once, then hands pull me out. I'm strapped to a board and rushed toward the whirling lights—red, white, red, white. The lights blind me, and I shut my eyes.

Doors slam and a siren screams. I have to squint because the lights are so bright. I shiver. The paramedics yell back and forth to each other and ask me questions I have a hard time focusing on. The pain in my chest spreads through my torso, and the slow-burning ache intensifies with each breath.

"Where are you hurting?" the woman asks.

"M-my chest." My throat feels like it's been scraped raw, and the words don't sound like me. They're too weak.

She cuts my shirt open. I want to cover myself, but my hands are strapped down. More questions fire at me. I try to focus. The lights are so bright, and the siren is so loud it isn't easy. A needle pricks my arm. They started an IV. Is it that serious? Other than the pain in my chest, I don't feel hurt.

"Do you remember what happened?"

"I-I was driving home from school. I'm a freshman at Ohio University." I swallow. My throat feels full of cotton.

"It was snowing and I lost control." My eyes search the woman's face, and I try to shake my head. "What did I hit?" Please don't let it be another car. I couldn't stand it if I'd hurt someone else.

"A tree."

Thank God.

"What's your name?" the other EMT asks.

I focus on him for the first time. His face is covered in acne. Is he old enough to be a paramedic? "Kara," I whisper. "Kara Jones."

By the time Mom shoves the white curtain aside I've been poked, X-rayed and seen by countless doctors and nurses.

"Kara! I was so worried!"

She rushes toward me, her face streaked with tears and her dark hair damp. Snowflakes still cling to some of the strands. Under the lights, they melt into tiny droplets that shimmer on her head like diamonds. She grabs my hand and rubs it against her cheek like she's trying to reassure herself I'm really here. The movement pulls at my IV, and the needle digs deeper. It's like a bruise spreading through my veins.

I wince, and she drops my hand. "I'm so sorry, baby. Did that hurt?"

She pets me like a cat. I resist the urge to push her hand away. Where's Dad? I need his calming presence. Mom makes me too nervous.

"Is Dad here?" I sound like someone who smokes a pack or two a day.

Mom bites her lower lip and flicks her hair out of her eyes. "He's parking the car."

She fidgets with the zipper on her jacket. Up, down, up, down. The *zip* is louder than the beeping of the medical equipment.

"I should go find the doctor." She keeps zipping. I wish she would go. "Did they tell you anything?"

"My ribs are bruised." Just breathing hurts, but talking is even worse. Every move causes pain to spread across my chest. "My spleen."

Mom gasps, and her face goes as white as snow.

"Ah, Mrs. Jones." The doctor comes in behind Mom. He's Indian, but he has a British accent. Young and cute. I probably look like crap right now. "I'm Dr. Patel."

Before Mom can start grilling the doctor, Dad walks in. His salt and pepper hair is matted and damp, and little drops of water glimmer on his glasses. But his gray eyes are focused on me, and he doesn't seem to notice.

"Kara!"

He stops halfway to my bed. His eyes travel over the tubes in my arms, going up to the bag that slowly drips liquid into my body. White-faced, he tugs at the sleeve of his jacket. It reminds me of something Mom would do.

"I'm okay."

He nods but doesn't move. My parents are both statues.

Dr. Patel clears his throat. "Kara is one lucky girl. She has some bruising to her ribs and spleen, but nothing more serious. We'll be admitting her for observation, and she could need a blood transfusion or two, but most likely it will heal on its own."

Mom swallows and her face turns an odd shade that isn't the least bit normal. Is she going to throw up? This is so typical of her. She didn't hear a single positive thing Dr. Patel had to say, only the negative. Thank God I take after Dad; her constant negativity drives me nuts.

"No surgery?" she asks in a shaky voice.

Dr. Patel is already inching toward the exit. "No, no. We try to avoid that these days. She really should just need rest, but we'll want to observe her to make sure something more serious doesn't happen."

"Like the spleen rupturing." Mom's words are barely

audible.

Dr. Patel stops and smiles, but it doesn't look sympathetic. His eyes move toward the curtain before going back to Mom. "Mrs. Jones, I don't think that's going to happen. In Kara's case, the damage does seem to be very minor." He clears his throat. "Now, if you don't have any further questions…" He looks back and forth between my parents, but neither one says a thing. "The nurse will be in soon to check on you."

He disappears without another word, and Dad finally manages to get his feet moving. He comes to my side and pats my arm, but he's not petting me the way Mom did. "You're not in too much pain?"

I shake my head, but even that makes me wince. The corners of Dad's mouth turn down and Mom looks away. Geez. That's the problem with being an only child—your parents' world revolves around you.

I suck in a deep breath and work on keeping my expression blank, so my parents can't see how much it hurts. "I'm fine," I manage to get out. "It hurts, but it's not serious." Mom starts crying. "Really, Mom, I'm good."

She nods and sniffs and comes over next to Dad. They stare down at me like I'm in a coffin, not a hospital bed. It makes me squirm, but even that hurts, so I have to stop.

"Hi!" The nurse comes in and I want to let out a sigh of relief, but it would hurt too much. "We're getting a room all ready for you upstairs. Hopefully, we'll be able to get you out of the ER soon. Okay?"

She's young—probably fresh out of nursing school—and wearing too much makeup for someone working in an emergency room. With the way her hair and face are made up she'd look more at home in a skimpy nurse uniform dancing at a bachelor party than here in a pair of green scrubs. A giggle bubbles up inside me, and I press my lips together to keep it from popping out. Mom frowns at me, but Dad's lips twitch like he knows what I'm thinking. It only makes me want to laugh even more. Of course, that would be stupid. If breathing hurts, laughing would probably make me pass out.

"The doctor said she might need a blood transfusion?" Mom is still playing with her zipper.

The nurse nods, picks up my chart, and scans it. Her lips press together, and her nose scrunches up like thinking hurts. It's probably all that blonde hair. I can make fun because my hair is black like Mom's.

When the nurse doesn't look up from the chart Mom frowns. "Can we donate?"

Blondie finally glances up and flashes a dazzling smile, like she's in a commercial for some drug company. "Of course. We always need blood donors."

"We're both O," Dad says.

Blondie's smile fades. She looks back down at the chart. Her face scrunches up even more as her eyes scan the paper, and Mom grips my hand. Her fingernails dig into my skin. I want to shake her off, but that would hurt too much. I wiggle my fingers and hope she'll get the point. She doesn't ease up.

"What's wrong?" Mom asks in a shaky voice.

Blondie looks up and arches an eyebrow. "Kara's adopted?"

My heart sputters like a dying motor. "What?" My voice is raspy again, only this time it has nothing to do with my injuries.

"No!" Mom's hand finally releases mine and goes to her throat. Her face goes two shades whiter. I didn't think it was possible.

I stare at them, waiting for an explanation. Dad shakes his head. Mom just shakes.

"No." Dad's voice is firm, but there's a small quiver to the word.

Blondie's eyes get huge, and she clears her throat. "Oh. My mistake." She stares at the floor.

Dad takes a small step away from Mom. "Why would you ask that?"

Blondie forces a smile and meets Dad's eyes. "Must be a mistake in the chart. No big deal. I'll look into it." She practically runs toward the curtain. "Let me check on your room."

The second she pulls the curtain shut, I turn on my parents. "I'm adopted!" My face is hot, and my breathing comes faster. It makes everything between my shoulders and waist ache, but I don't care. How could they have kept this from me?

Mom smiles, but it's so tight it's more like a grimace. "Of course you're not. You've seen pictures of me when I was pregnant."

That's true. Still, what the hell was that all about? "Why would she say that?"

Mom's hands shake. Dad stares at the floor. "You heard her. Just a mistake." She clears her throat, and her eyes flit toward the curtain. "Let me go see what the confusion was. Maybe they got your chart mixed up with someone else's. I don't want there to be any more problems." She's already walking toward the curtain. She hasn't looked at Dad once.

"Dad?"

He looks up, and his gray eyes move over my face like he's seeing me for the first time. My chest tightens, and it's as if I'm right back in that car with the steering wheel pressed against me. Why does it seem like something awful is about to happen?

"It was a mistake." He kicks at the floor and shoves his hands in his pockets. "I'm going to go check on your mom."

He doesn't close the curtain all the way, and I spot Mom at the nurse's station. Her face is red as she yells at the nurse. She never yells. The nurse is crying. What the hell is happening?

The color drains from Mom's face when Dad walks up. My throat tightens. They start to argue, and the nurses gathered around stare like they're watching their favorite soap. Tears stream down Mom's face when she reaches for Dad, and the terror inside me increases when he brushes her off. Dad glances my way once before turning around. He walks away, down the longest hallway I've ever seen. It gets longer, and the edges of my vision grow dark. The temperature shoots up sixty degrees in a matter of seconds until I can't watch anymore. My head sways and the darkness closes in, and I let it.

CHAPTER TWO

I ease into the wheelchair as slowly as I can, but it doesn't help. Everything aches. Mom hovers over me, wringing her hands. She's been like this for the past two days. Forty-eight hours trapped in a tiny hospital room with her. All I want to do is escape.

"Why don't you go pull the car up?" I snap.

Mom winces and the nurse frowns, but I don't care. I'm suffocating here. She won't tell me anything about Dad and all she does is hover over me. I need a break.

"O-okay. I'll meet you by the front door." Her voice shakes and a twinge of regret shoots through me. But it's miniscule.

Mom grabs my bag, flicks her dark hair out of her face, and looks at me one last time before heading toward the door. When she's finally gone, I relax.

The nurse goes over my discharge instructions and her eyes snap whenever she looks at me. She thinks I'm a bitch. All I've heard the last few days is how lucky I am to have a mother so dedicated. How wonderful it is that she hasn't left my side. I'm sure I seem ungrateful, but they don't know. The drama unfolded in the ER. The nurses on this floor have no clue. Not that I do either. Mom won't tell me a thing, and it pisses me off. She keeps saying I'm too sick; we can worry about it after I'm recovered. How am I supposed to ignore the fact my dad has disappeared?

By the time the volunteer shows up to push me downstairs, I can't wait to escape the nurse's judgment. The hospital walls are decorated with red garlands and there are Christmas lights around the doors. *Jingle Bells* rings out through the overhead speakers, and we pass an artificial tree set up next to the nurse's station. Christmas is four days away, but it feels more like we're approaching the apocalypse than the most wonderful time of the year.

The volunteer chats away behind me, oblivious to the fact that I'm not answering, telling me all about his grandchildren coming in from Iowa. My head aches, and I can't wait to escape the tiny elevator. He's being nice, but I just want him to shut up.

The music on the first floor is even louder. When we approach the front door, I see why. Carolers. If they're not careful, I'm going to snap and tell them where they can shove their Christmas cheer.

The glass doors slide open and icy air rushes in. It's snowing still, but rock salt has been sprinkled across the sidewalk and pavement to keep the ice away. The snow that hasn't melted is gray and dirty, polluted. That's how I feel. My insides are dark and grimy. This isn't how my first Christmas home from college was supposed to be. The volunteer blabbers on while we wait for Mom, and I shiver. Why couldn't we have waited inside? Every time my body shakes the pain in my chest grows.

After what seems like ages, Mom pulls up in front of me. She jumps out of the driver's side and rushes around the front of her silver Accord, like if she doesn't get here fast enough I'm going to disappear. Not the case. She has me trapped now. No car, no cell phone since it was smashed in the wreck, bed rest for at least two weeks. I am her prisoner.

Mom grabs my arm when I start to stand. I really want to push her away, but my chest and left side hurt too bad. My freaking spleen better heal fast or I won't make it. She'll suffocate me.

"Careful, Kara." She helps me ease into the passenger seat.

"Thanks," I manage. I'm mad, but I have to admit I hurt too much to do it on my own.

She shuts the door, and while she runs to the other side, I get a few precious seconds to myself to gather my thoughts. There's been a lot to process the last two days, and I've had almost no time alone. But it isn't long enough. She's at the driver's side in seconds, sliding into the car, glancing at me while she fiddles with the keys.

I only give her long enough to start the engine before I ask, "Is Dad home?"

Her jaw tightens. She doesn't say a word until she pulls onto the road, and we're heading home. "I don't know."

"What do you mean? I want to know what's going on!" The past two days have been nothing but questions from me and cryptic answers from her, and it's making my head hurt. I try to turn so I'm facing her, but pain shoots up my left side, and I have to stop. "Please," I say through clenched teeth.

"We can worry about all that later. You're hurt and right now you need to focus on getting better. I don't want to upset you." She keeps her eyes on the road, and her hands clench the steering wheel so tight that if she were any stronger, she'd rip it off.

My neck is hot. The heat creeps up my cheeks. "You're upsetting me already. Can't you see that? I want to know why my dad hasn't come to see me. I want to know what you two are fighting about that's so bad he couldn't even call to see if I was okay!"

"He called your nurse twice a day."

"But he didn't come to see me."

She licks her lips, and her hands tighten even more.

"We'll talk about it later."

I turn my face away from her and stare out the passenger window. We don't say another word, and I pretend she isn't there. The world flies by as we leave Dayton and head into Englewood. By the time we turn onto our street, my head hurts from watching the houses and businesses whiz past me, but I can't look away.

When Mom pulls into the driveway, she gasps. Dad is sitting on the porch. It would be a comforting sight if we didn't have six inches of snow on the ground. Instead of being excited, I'm filled with a sense of dread that weighs my stomach down and makes the runny eggs I ate this morning threaten to come back up.

I throw the door open the second the car is in park and try to pull myself out. My chest and side pound, but I keep moving.

Dad is in front of me before I've managed to hoist myself out of the car completely. "Careful, honey." He puts his arm around my waist and helps me stand.

"Dad!" I want to hug him. I want to throw my arms around him and squeeze him until we both can't breathe, but I hold back. No matter what Mom did, I can't understand why he would abandon me like that. I'm his daughter! "Where have you been?"

A puff of steam floats out of his mouth and drifts off into the sky. "Let's go inside."

"Greg," Mom says in a shaky voice. "You're coming in?"

We both turn. She stands by the driver's side, gripping the door tightly. Her eyes shine with hope.

"For a few minutes," Dad says, and Mom's face crumbles.

Once we're inside, he helps me to the couch. His glasses fog up and he has to take them off so he can wipe them on his sweater. He isn't wearing a jacket. How was he sitting out there with no jacket on? It's December in Ohio. He had to be freezing!

Mom stands in the doorway, her arms crossed over her chest and her black hair a mess. The sloppiness isn't like her; she's typically so put together. But Mom isn't who I need to be focusing on right now. I've been asking her what's going on for two days, and I've gotten nowhere. Dad will tell me.

I put my back to her and focus on Dad's face. "Why didn't you come see me?"

He rubs the back of his neck. "I'm sorry, honey. I should have I just…" He sighs and pinches his nose the way he does when he's stressed. "I couldn't be around her right now. It's too hard."

I take a deep breath, willing myself to stay in control. "Why? What's happened?"

Dad's gray eyes move to Mom. "You didn't tell her, Charlotte?"

Mom's shoulders slump even more. "She was hurt. I didn't want to add any undue stress."

He puts his head in his hands and digs his fingers into his scalp like he's trying to crush his own skull. "You should have told her eighteen years ago." The words hiss through his teeth. "You should have told me."

"What's going on?" I gasp for breath between the words. I'm close to hyperventilating.

Dad's eyes meet mine. They are so full of pain. "What the nurse said…"

My mouth pops open. "I *am* adopted."

He winces. "No."

"I don't understand. What, then? What's happening?" My stomach feels like it's full of rocks.

"Your blood type is AB." Every word makes his face scrunch up even more. "Your mom and I are both O." He looks away when I shake my head. I still don't understand. "There's no way I could be your father."

The room spins and I want to curl up in a ball, but I can't move. My heart. I grab my chest and squeeze. Mom steps forward with her hand out. One look from me and she stops.

"What?" The word is so quiet I'm not even sure I said it.

Dad takes my hand. The one that isn't trying to hold my heart together. "I'm still your father."

"But you're not? Not really?"

He shakes his head, and I blink. Tears drop from my eyes onto my legs, leaving dark circles on my jeans. This can't be real. Things like this don't really happen, right? Not to normal families like ours. Not to one of the few couples who are actually happy together and still in love after twenty years of marriage.

"You didn't know?" I can't look at Mom, so I focus on Dad's eyes. When he shakes his head, my stomach convulses and jumps to my throat.

I turn to Mom. "You knew?"

She doesn't even try to deny it or defend herself. All she does is stand there, staring at us with those unflinching blue eyes of hers. Mine are the same color, but they have more life in them. I've always attributed that to my dad. What a joke!

"I have your personality!" My voice shakes and I want to get up and run away, but my body is too battered to make an escape. I do stand up. "You!" I scream at Mom. "You cheated on Dad? How could you? And to lie about it all these years!"

She finally cracks. Tears fall from her eyes, and she takes a step toward me. I back away. Pain shoots through my body. At this point, I don't know if it's physical or emotional.

"It's not what you think," she says. "We were split up."

"Charlotte, stop it," Dad says.

"What? It's true!"

Dad shakes his head. "We broke up for one month. You were cheating on me long before that. You only came crawling back when you found out you were pregnant. I was an easy target." He sounds so bitter. I can't blame him.

"What do you mean you broke up? You mean you got separated?"

Mom's shoulders slump. "I was pregnant when we got married."

I shake my head and she puts her hand up to stop me. Why does she look so calm and put together suddenly? All those times she's fallen apart over the tiniest things, and now when the world is crashing down around me, she's as cool as a cucumber, whatever that means.

"We told you we got married two years before you were born. That isn't true. We were dating, and I met someone else. I didn't mean to cheat; it just happened. For a time, I thought I wanted to be with him, but it didn't turn out well. When I found out I was pregnant I went back to your father." She turns her eyes on Dad, but he won't look at her. "I didn't know then! Not for sure. She could have just as easily been your baby."

"But you found out later."

Mom nods, but there's no way he can see.

My legs shake. I sink back onto the couch just as Dad gets to his feet. He puts his hand on my shoulder, and I stare up at him. He isn't looking at me, and he isn't looking at Mom. He's staring at the door. One squeeze of my shoulder and he's gone, pushing past Mom without even glancing her way. The wind howls when he opens the front door, and when it slams shut my heart splits in two.

CHAPTER THREE

The walls vibrate from when my dad slammed the door. It's more violent than an earthquake.

Or is that me?

I have to blink a few times to get my eyes to focus. My legs shake and every tiny tremor that runs through my body makes me ache even more. I dig my fingers into my knees to keep them from knocking together, but it's pointless. My hands are shaking, too.

The silence in the room is so thick it chokes me. I swallow, but it takes a lot more effort than it should. Like a golf ball is lodged in my throat. She's watching me. Her eyes are more intense than a laser beam. I can't force myself to meet them.

My head pounds. I abandon my shaky legs and massage my temples, keeping my eyes down. Anything, so I don't have to look at her. "Where's my real father?"

"It's not important."

I look up even though I don't want to. "What?"

Mom twists a strand of dark hair around her finger. "You don't want to know him, trust me."

She sinks into the overstuffed armchair like her legs are

about to give out. Still twisting the hair. Over and over it circles her fingers until she releases it and starts again.

"I deserve to know where I came from," I whisper. I don't even have the energy to yell.

Mom sinks deeper into the chair. "Sometimes a lie is better than the truth. Believe me."

"Trust you? Believe you?" My face gets hot. Maybe I have the energy after all. "I'll *never* be able to do that again! You've lied to me my whole life. To Dad! Everything has been a lie!"

"No, it hasn't. Your dad will see that soon. He'll come around."

She's crazy. I saw the look in his eyes. He's devastated. A person doesn't come back from something like this. "How can you think that?"

She finally looks at me, and her blue eyes shimmer with unshed tears. "What about your life has been a lie? One thing. One tiny, insignificant thing. I love you. Your Dad loves you. We've been happy. He *is* your father in every single way but one. How can this matter that much?"

I ball up my hands into fists and press them against my temples while I try to process the words coming out of her mouth. "You lied. That's what matters. Dad will always be my dad—biology can't change that. But I want to know where I came from. What can be so awful that you can't tell me that?"

"Kara," Mom says softly, "once you learn something you can never unlearn it. If I tell you the truth, it will change your life."

Something feels wrong about her words. I turn them over and over in my head, studying them. Trying to make some sense out of this whole thing. "What is it? Where you raped?"

Mom shakes her head. "No. I was very much in love with your father."

I exhale, trying to ignore the pain that splinters across my chest when I do. "Then he was abusive? An alcoholic?

What?"

She shakes her head again and looks through me like she's staring into the past. "I don't want to talk about this anymore."

"But I do!" I jump to my feet, and pain bursts through me. Stars explode behind my eyes, blinding me, and I double over, gripping my side. That only makes it worse.

"Kara!"

Mom is by my side, and I don't push her away because I genuinely need the help. I'm too drained to do it on my own. She helps me up to my room, and by the time we get there my body is covered in sweat. I hate that I need her.

"I'm not done talking about this," I whisper while she helps me change into more comfortable clothes.

She won't look at me. "Just rest for now."

Mom helps me into bed, and I don't fight her. I curl up into a ball and close my eyes to block out everything that just happened. Trying to forget that my dad is not my dad, and there's a man somewhere who helped give me life. That he's too much of a jerk or too evil or too broken for my mom to want to me to know who he is.

Christmas morning in the living room, surrounded by presents. Just like my last eighteen Christmases. The lights on the tree twinkle and there's a thick blanket of snow on the ground. The smooth voice of Bing Crosby plays in the other room, reminding us he'll be home for Christmas. It should be the perfect setting. Only it isn't because Dad is missing, and my mood is so bitter I can taste it. Even the cinnamon rolls and hot chocolate Mom forces on me can't cover it up.

I want to know where Dad is, but he hasn't called. Even worse, Mom still refuses to tell me who my biological father is. Whenever I ask she clamps her lips together and leaves the room. Like I'm the one at fault.

"I want to call Dad," I say, ignoring the present Mom tries to hand me. I don't want to open them, not without Dad here. "Let me use your phone."

Mom lowers the brightly wrapped package. "Let's wait until after we open the presents."

"No. Now."

She sighs and heads into the other room to get her phone. I chew on the inside of my cheek. Where could he be staying? We don't have any family, not nearby, anyway. Both Mom's and Dad's parents are dead, and Mom was an only child. Dad has a brother in Florida, but there's no way he would go there. They aren't exactly close. A hotel, I guess. Possibly a friend's house. Although, all of Dad's friends are Mom's friends too. That might make things uncomfortable.

When Mom comes back with the phone, I struggle to my feet. My side and chest ache, but it's not as intense as it was a few days ago. Hopefully, my body heals fast.

I take the phone and head into the kitchen.

"Where are you going?"

"I need privacy," I snap. Should she really be surprised?

I lean against the kitchen counter while the phone rings. Once. Twice. Three times. Voicemail. He must have hit the ignore button. Not a surprise—this is Mom's number. Why would he want to talk to her? All I have to do is leave a message. He'll call me back. He has to.

"Dad, it's Kara. I'm on Mom's phone because mine broke in the wreck. I'm going to try to get a new one in a few days. Call me back on this. I'll make sure Mom doesn't answer. I miss you. It's Christmas." My voice catches, and I have to clear my throat before I can go on. "I want to see you."

I push end, but don't move. There's nowhere for me to go.

"He'll call. He'll come around. You'll see."

I jump and spin around to face her, but the movement is too fast. I grab my side. It feels like my spleen is pulsating. "I think you're delusional," I say through clenched teeth.

"We'll see." She tilts her head toward the living room. "Let's open the presents."

"No. I'm going upstairs to lie down. I don't want to open them without Dad."

I hold my side as I push past her. Beads of sweat break out on my forehead. If it wasn't for this damn spleen, I'd just leave. Head out on foot and walk to a friend's house. Megan lives only four miles away. Who cares if there's snow?

But I can't do that, not with the way things are right now, so I go up to my room and crawl into bed. My hand is wrapped so tightly around Mom's phone that I'm surprised it doesn't break in two. I lie there, staring at it. Willing it to ring.

But it doesn't, and by noon, my chest is so tight that I feel like I'm back in that car. Trapped. I can't breathe. The phone taunts me with its silence.

Mom's background picture is of the three of us at my graduation. I'm wearing a green cap and gown, smiling with an arm around each of my parents. My eyes narrow on the picture. I study my face then compare it to my parents'. Mom looks like one of those age progression pictures of me. Our eyes are the same blue and our hair is raven black, thanks to her bi-monthly trips to the salon. We have the same oval face and almond-shaped eyes, turned up just slightly at the corners. We're even almost the same height. I have an inch on her. If it wasn't for my mouth, we'd look exactly alike, but our smiles are different. My lips are fuller and my mouth just a little too big for my face. She has dimples in both cheeks, and I have none.

Then there's Dad. There's nothing in his face that resembles me. Should it have been a red flag? No. That's insane. I know a lot of people who don't look like their parents. It doesn't mean anything.

Only in my case, it does.

A knock on the door makes me jump. "Kara."

I do the mature thing: roll over and cover my face with my blanket. The position makes my ribs throb, and I have to bite down on my bottom lip and squeeze my eyes shut until it subsides. I will not give her the satisfaction of getting up.

"Kara!" Her voice gets a bit louder and there's a hint of frustration to it.

The doorknob rattles, but I stay under the blanket. It's locked. Will she have the nerve to open it? At this point, I wouldn't put anything past her.

Mom's sigh is so deep it penetrates the door, the covers, and the arm I have draped over my head. She stops calling me, and she stops trying to open the door. After a second her footsteps move down the hall. I'm glad she's gone, but now that I'm alone the silence is even more constricting than the steering wheel was. There's no one for me to talk to. Some of my friends are probably home for the holidays, but without my phone I'm lost. All their numbers were stored in my cell. Why was I so stupid I never thought to write them down on an actual piece of paper? Mom *has* to take me to get a phone tomorrow. I won't let her make excuses. And a car! I need a way to escape.

It's December twenty-fifth and classes don't start again until mid-January. No way I can wait that long. I'll have to think of an excuse to get out of here earlier.

I open my eyes to darkness, and the air filling my lungs is thick and stale. The blanket is still over my head. When I pull it down the room doesn't get any brighter. How long have I been asleep?

I flip on Mom's phone and the screen lights up. It's after seven o'clock. My stomach growls. If it were possible, I'd stay in this room by myself forever rather than face her.

But sooner or later I'm going to have to leave. Might as well be now.

When I peak my head into the hallway, it's silent. There's no light on in the hall or at the bottom of the stairs. Is she sitting alone in a dark room just staring at the wall? There's no way she's in bed already; it's too early.

I creep down the stairs and when I reach the bottom, the only light is the twinkling of the Christmas tree. I take a deep breath, step into the living room, and freeze. Mom's sitting on the couch. But she doesn't react, and when I step closer I notice the empty bottle of wine next to her. There isn't even a glass. Classy.

A photo album sits next to her, and my gut hardens and twists. No. I will not feel bad for her. She lied. And what's worse, she's still doing it! She isn't going to give in; I know her. She's stubborn. Guess I got that from her.

My legs wobble and I lean against the doorframe. There has to be a way to find out who my father is. Maybe she told someone. A friend or something. My parents started dating when Mom was in grad school, and Dad was teaching English at the local high school. They met through mutual friends, but as far as I know they don't keep in touch with anyone from college. At least, I've never met anyone they knew when they lived in Kent.

She says she loved this man. Maybe she kept some kind of memento? But where? Not where Dad would find it. That would be stupid.

My stomach growls, but I ignore it and focus on Mom. She's really out. Her head is back, and her mouth is wide open. She won't be waking up for a while. I have to do it now.

I dash up the stairs as fast as my bruised ribs and spleen will take me, which is about as fast as an eighty-year-old woman, and head for Mom and Dad's room. Mom's room now. I'm not stupid; he won't be back. But does that mean he's leaving me too? I shove the thought out of my head. I can't focus on that right now. There's nothing I can do about it, so I might as well focus on something I can control: ransacking Mom's room in search of evidence.

I flip the light switch and both lamps come on. It's blinding after the darkness of the house, and it takes me a few seconds of squinting before I'm able to see clearly. Now I just have to decide where to look. The nightstand? No, too obvious. Dresser? Not likely, but maybe at the back of one of the drawers.

I pull open the first drawer and shove her underwear around, not caring that I'm making a mess. There's nothing there, so I do the same with the next, and the next. Other than an old birthday card from my grandma, her drawers don't have anything in them but clothes.

Okay, so the dresser was a bust. Where else? A box in the closet? She has a bunch on the shelves.

When I flip the light on, I do my best not to focus on how painfully empty Dad's side is. The closet is huge, and the shelves are all lined with boxes, most labeled by my OCD mother. Makes this whole thing a lot easier.

I scan the labels. They say things like *Kara Baby Clothes*, *Kara Elementary School*, *Kara Middle School*, *Kara High School*. God, it's like a weird shrine to me in here. And it *doesn't* make me feel the least bit guilty. Not…at…all.

Focus. *Mom and Dad*—nope. Grandma and grandpa wouldn't have had anything to do with it. *Childhood Memories*—nope. *Pictures*—maybe. It's possible she has some in there from college, but unless she wrote *Kara's Father* on the back of one, it isn't going to help. *College*—bingo! That has to tell me something!

There's a step stool folded up behind Dad's suits, and my hands start to shake when I pull it out, and get a whiff of his cologne. *Stop it, Kara. You can't think about that.*

My side and chest throb when I climb the ladder, and it only gets worse when I reach for the box, but I jam my teeth into my bottom lip and work through it. My face is beaded with sweat, by the time I step down, but the box is firmly in my hands.

I ease myself down in the middle of the closet and rip the lid off. It's full of Kent State memorabilia. There are two small photo albums on top. I pull those out first and set them aside. They'll only be helpful if they're carefully labeled—which, knowing my mom, they might be—but I want to see what else is in here before I deal with that. A stack of playbills, a few concert ticket stubs. A Kent State sweatshirt that smells like…I put it to my nose and take a deep whiff, and my eyebrows shoot up. Pot! Mom, you bad girl. My lips curl up into a smile before I remember I'm mad at her. Damn. I've never been as close to her as I have been to Dad, but we don't fight. Not like this. I'll think about that later. Not now.

I turn back to the box. There's a bound copy of her thesis—not something I'm going to read—and under that a few more papers. Then nothing. The sweatshirt took up most of the box. Shit. I thought for sure I'd find something. But there's nothing here with any actual names on it.

That leaves the photo albums. Hopefully, Mom was as OCD back then as she is now. I flip the first one open and exhale. The pictures are labeled. Thank you, Mom.

I turn page after page, studying the pictures. It seems to be the same eight people over and over again. Mom, Dad, a blonde girl named Liz, a redhead named Grace, an Asian girl named Tobi, and three guys. Could one of them be my father? Mark, Brad and Jeff. No last names for anyone. How am I going to find out who these people are? A yearbook would be nice, but of course that would be too much to hope for. Crap.

I lean my head back and wrack my brain. What's my next step? There would be a yearbook in the university library, but Kent State is four hours away, and I don't have a car anymore. Plus, it's the holidays, so they're closed. I'll have to make a trip up there in a few months. Well shit! How can I go months with this hanging over my head?

There's no way I'll be able to sleep. I'm going to get an ulcer.

But I don't have another option, so I put the box back—minus the photo albums—and replace the step stool. After a quick pit stop in my room to stash the albums, I head downstairs to grab something to eat.

CHAPTER FOUR

The sun is barely up when I walk into the kitchen. Mom is drinking her coffee. Probably nursing a hangover after last night's bottle of wine. She isn't dressed yet, and her hair is messy and knotted. The considerate thing would be to wait until she's had time to really wake up. But I'm starting to feel trapped, so I don't.

"You have to take me to get a new phone."

Mom barely looks up. "What?"

"I need a new phone. All of my friend's numbers were in that phone and I can't call any of them. They have no idea I was in an accident!"

Mom sips her coffee, making a slurping sound that is much louder than it needs to be. The hair on the back of my neck stands up, and I clench my fists. Is she doing it on purpose? Trying to irritate me? No. What would be the point? I'm already pissed.

I swallow down my frustration. "Please."

Mom nods once then squeezes her eyes shut. "Okay. Give me an hour."

An hour later, I'm standing by the front door with my arms crossed over my chest when my mom comes down the stairs. She's changed into a pair of yoga pants and one of Dad's sweatshirts. It's huge on her. Her hair is pulled into a ponytail, and she has dark circles under her eyes. I'm not sure she's slept at all since Dad left. Other than last night, which was really more like passing out. Her eyes meet mine and even though she grabs her head when she does it, she smiles. It makes my heart tremble. Dammit. I need to give her a break. I'm never going to understand why she did what she did, but she obviously felt like she had good reasons. And she's hurting. No matter what happened in the past, she loves Dad. I've never seen love like theirs. Never.

She tilts her head to the side. "You sure you're up to this?"

"I need a phone." I'm not going to let her talk me out of going. If I don't find someone to talk to soon I'm going to lose it.

She presses her lips together, her usual worried expression. "Honey, you were in a car accident less than a week ago. If you're in too much pain it can wait."

"I'm okay as long as I don't move my upper body."

Mom sighs. "Let's go."

When I climb into the car, I'm so jittery that I'm almost visibly shaking. It isn't something I expected. I must have been too distracted thinking about my dad when we'd left the hospital, but now as Mom backs out of the driveway, I break out into a cold sweat. Images of the accident flash through my mind. I clench my fists when I remember what it was like to have the steering wheel pressed up against me.

I inhale slowly through my nose and push the air back out through my mouth, then wait for my body to calm down. The streets are packed with post-holiday shoppers, and I say a silent thank you we don't have to go to the mall. There's no way I'd have the energy to fight a crowd.

Mom's hands are on ten and two, just like they always are when she drives. Her knuckles are white from gripping the steering wheel. "How are your ribs feeling?"

I press my lips together. There's a part of me that really doesn't want to talk to her, but I did decide I needed to be nicer. It will help get what I want out of her, too: information and a new car. The first one would be nice even if it is a long shot, but the second one is a must. I need a car so I can get back to school.

I clear my throat. "I'm sore, but it's getting better. I just have to remember not to move much."

The corner of Mom's mouth turns up. "That doesn't sound too difficult." Her fingers wring the steering wheel. "So, how was school going? No boyfriends?"

"Boyfriends?" I have to laugh. "You think I should have more than one?"

She smiles, an actual real smile. The corner of her eyes crinkle, and her laugh lines deepen in a way that makes her face soften. She really is a beautiful woman. Thank God I look like her. I have the same dark hair and blue eyes. I'm not ashamed to say I think I'm pretty. It's confidence, not vanity.

But I wonder what features I got from my father...

No matter how hard I try I can't stop from asking, "You're never going to tell me, are you?"

Her smile fades. "No."

I sniff and try to keep my voice from shaking. "Just think about it, okay?"

"I'm not going to change my mind."

Of course not. I stare out the window, and the pain in my chest builds until it becomes something more volatile. Anger, hurt and regret, all rolled into a ball that clouds my vision. I blink, but it doesn't help.

"I need a new car," I blurt out. Mom's mouth opens, but before she can say anything I continue, "I know you haven't gotten the insurance money yet, but I really need a car, so I can go back to school after New Year's."

She grips the steering wheel tighter. "You're not going back."

"What?" I turn to face her too fast and end up blinded by pain, but even that can't overshadow the confusion. There's no way I heard her right.

"I withdrew you."

I stare at her, but she won't look away from the damn road. "Why would you do that?"

"You were hurt. You need time to recover."

"Two weeks!" She flinches, but there's nothing she could do right now to make me feel bad. "I'll be fine by the time the spring semester starts. How could you do this to me?"

"With everything going on, I just thought it would be best. You need time to deal with all this stuff, not just the accident." She still won't look at me.

I grip my jeans like I'm trying to rip them off my legs. "You're punishing me for something *you* did!"

"Kara." Her voice is too calm; it makes me want to hit her, and I have to tighten my grip on my jeans. "You need time to deal with all this."

"How can I when you won't tell me a thing?" I spit at her.

She doesn't respond. Either she doesn't have an answer, or she knows anything she says will only make it worse. Either way, I'm glad she stays silent. I don't want to hear what she has to say to me anyway.

I'm shaking again. Mostly from anger, but also from hurt. Betrayal and pain are mixed in there too. And other emotions so new to me I don't even have names for them. Things have never been this tense between me and my mom, and I have no idea how to cope. All this emotion and pent-up disappointment are starting to make me feel crushed. Insignificant.

"Take me home." The tears have started flowing and there's no way I'll be able to stop them long enough to get a phone.

CHAPTER FIVE

Two weeks. That's all I can think when I open my eyes. Today is two weeks since my accident. Christmas came and went. New Year's Eve had me hiding in my room, and here it is, the first day of 2015. It really is a new year. My dad isn't my dad. I haven't spoken to him in more than a week, and I have no idea where he is. I'll never know who my real father is, I'm collegeless, carless, and phoneless, and there isn't a single person I can call to talk to about it all. Happy New Year!

I want to cry.

After I've gotten ready for the day, I head downstairs. Mom is banging around in the kitchen, and the air is thick with the greasy scent of bacon. My stomach growls even though I'm not a breakfast person. Traitor.

"Happy New Year," Mom calls.

I freeze in my tracks, halfway through the living room. What now? I haven't spoken to her since we drove home from our failed cell phone attempt six days ago. My New Year's resolution was to forgive her, though. Does that mean I have to do it today? Or does it mean I have until the end of the year?

I'm going to go with the second one.

I walk into the kitchen, but refuse even to look at her. Coffee. That's what I need to focus on right now. Not Mom, not Dad, not the mystery man who gave me life. Coffee.

And then how the hell I'm going to get out of this house.

"So, you're still giving me the silent treatment?" Even though I'm not looking directly at her, I can see her out of the corner of my eye. Her hands are on her hips, and her mouth is all scrunched up.

But I won't give in. I sip my coffee and walk back toward the stairs. Shower time.

"You're going to have to talk to me eventually! We live in the same house," she shouts after me.

I choke on my coffee.

I stare out the bay window with my third cup of coffee clutched in my hand. Drinking it is stupid. It's almost five o'clock and if I have any more caffeine, I may explode. I take another sip.

It's snowing again. Dammit. Why does it keep snowing?

Mom is in the kitchen humming like crazy. She's been humming that same tune nonstop since our fight six days ago, when I stopped talking to her. I'm not sure if she's trying to wear me down by annoying the shit out of me, or she's just doing it so she can forget how awful things are. Either way, all I want to do is run down the street screaming. The walls are getting closer and closer together. I swear it's true. I'm not making it up. Yesterday this room was twice as big. At least.

"Dinner will be done in about ten minutes," she sings. Her voice is way too cheerful to be in this house.

That's all it takes. I slam my cup on the end table, not

caring that it sloshes over the edge, and march toward the door. My snow boots are sitting there, and it takes three seconds to slip them on. I rip the door open and dash outside. No jacket, no purse, no cell phone. I don't care about any of it. I just need to get away.

"Kara!"

I start to run. It hurts, but I don't care. Mom's voice echoes after me but I keep going. Down the street and around the corner. I don't slow until I make it out to the main road. There are no sidewalks here, but we're not that far from a dinky shopping center, so I run in the snow. It comes almost to the top of my boots. My nose and cheeks are frozen. My hands tingle, and every time I exhale a puff of steam rises up in front of me, but I keep going.

When my feet hit pavement, I slide a little and slow down. I can't get hurt right now, not when I'm finally feeling better. I need to work on relaxing, taking it easy, and getting well so I can get out of the house.

I scan the signs and pray something is open on New Year's Day. All the businesses are dark but one. A pool hall. I'd forgotten it was there. I've only been in it one time—it wasn't that impressive—but right now I just need to get someplace warm.

A bell chimes when I push the door open. Not an electric one, but a real one that hangs above the door. The room is dimly lit but thankfully not smoky, and pool tables are set up to the right. There's a bar to the left, and I head that way. When I'm halfway there it occurs to me that I don't have a wallet. No money. Son of a bitch!

I flop onto one of the barstools, and I have to resist the urge to lay my head on the counter. Suddenly, just sitting up seems like too much effort. A man and woman sit at the other end of the bar, whispering over foamy glasses of beer, but otherwise, the place is empty. Most people are probably at home nursing hangovers from last night. There are still pieces of confetti on the floor. They probably had a busy evening.

A man with a long, gray beard spots me and nods, but he doesn't come over. He looks like a pirate, the way his beard hangs to the middle of his chest, and his right eye squints when he looks at me. It's kind of funny. If I had any sense of humor left in my soul I'd laugh. Gray Beard—that's his pirate name for sure—elbows the guy next to him and tilts his head my way. I guess he doesn't like people? Odd line of work.

The other guy tosses a towel onto the bar and turns around. He's got to be around my age, and he looks a little familiar. He's tall and lean, lanky but not awkward, with dark hair that's slightly too long. It hangs across his eyebrows, and he has to flip his head to get it out of the way. His eyes are big and brown. And gorgeous.

"What can I get you?" He stops and cocks his head to the side. The corner of his mouth twitches. "Kara, right? Kara Jones?"

I do know him. How?

"Um…yeah." Wow, I feel like an ass. I have no idea what this guy's name is.

He leans against the bar and grins, revealing a set of perfect white teeth and a panty-dropping smile. He doesn't seem the least bit bothered that I don't know him. "Derek Miller."

"Oh." It sounds familiar, but my brain isn't really working right now.

He laughs and flips his hair out of his eyes again. "We went to high school together."

Wow. What a sexy smile. How do I not remember this guy? High school? I thought I knew every hot guy in school, but this guy…I have no idea who he is.

"I'm sorry," I say. "You look so familiar, but I just don't remember—"

He waves his hand in the air. "Don't worry about it. It was a big school. I only remember you because…" He pauses. "Never mind."

Okay, now I *really* want to know what he's thinking. I

lean forward and put my hand on his arm. His eyes go down, and the grin gets even bigger. I had no idea that was possible. "No," I say, "not 'never mind.' You started it, now you have to finish."

Derek rubs the back of his neck, and his cheeks turn red. "Seriously?" I nod. "Okay, you asked for it. We had chemistry together." I raise an eyebrow, and he laughs. "I mean the class."

I knew what he meant, but he is sooo cute when he grins. That little dimple in his right cheek—I could just curl up in it and go to sleep. "Go on," I say with a smile. Am I flirting? I am! How did I go from being ready to throw myself in front of a train to actually flirting?

"You sat in front of me, and sometimes when you leaned forward I could see your thong sticking out of the top of your pants."

My eyes bug out of my head. "I had no idea! You sat right behind me?" Now I feel like a total ass! Then again, I had chemistry junior year and that was when I was dating Bill Harper. I remember very little from that entire year.

"I'm so sorry." My hand is still on his arm. I don't move it. I need some kind of distraction, and Derek Miller seems like the answer to my prayers.

His brown eyes move back down to my hand for a brief second before going back to my face. "Don't be. It was hot."

Now it's my turn to laugh. "I meant for not remembering you. That whole year was kind of a blur— young love and all." That's not exactly accurate, but the last thing I need right now is to dredge up more painful memories.

"Right. Billy whatshisname."

"Bill Harper," I correct him. "He hated Billy."

Derek flashes me an adorable grin. "Well, I hated him, so that makes us even."

My cheeks ache from smiling, but I can't stop. There's something about this guy that is so unbelievably relaxing.

If they could bottle him, they'd make millions—forget Zoloft.

Gray Beard clears his throat, and Derek stands up, finally moving so my hand is no longer resting on his arm. "So what can I get you, *Kara Jones*?"

A shiver runs down my spine. There's something about the way he says my name; it's like a caress.

"I would love a drink, but I can't for two reasons. One, you know I'm not twenty-one, and two, I don't have any money."

"No money?" He rests his elbow back on the bar like he's settling in. I wish he would. He's making me forget everything that's happened the last two weeks.

"I ran out of the house without my wallet."

His brown eyes sparkle. "Now there has to be a story behind that."

Do I talk about it or not? On one hand, I've been dying to talk to someone about it, but on the other hand I was just starting to forget how miserable the last two weeks have been.

"You can tell me. I'm a bartender." I raise an eyebrow, and Derek leans forward until our faces are only a few inches apart. "Well, not officially. Officially, I take care of the billiards part of the business." He winks, and I giggle. Like a little schoolgirl!

When he smiles again my heart actually skips a few beats. "I really don't have any money."

His smile fades and his brown eyes sweep over my face. "You okay?"

How did he know? Probably, because I look like crap. I haven't exactly been sleeping well. "I've been better…"

Derek drums his fingers on the counter. "How 'bout this? I'll start you a tab—just between you and me—and when you find that wallet of yours, you stop in. How's that sound?"

I lean closer and lower my voice so no one else can hear. "Um…I'm not exactly twenty-one."

The corner of his mouth turns up. "Like I said, just between you and me."

I exhale and my shoulders actually relax. They've been in knots for two weeks. "That would be amazing."

Three drinks, and I tell him about the accident. Five, and I'm spilling my guts. Derek sits on the stool next to me—he must have finished his shift—hanging on my every word as I relate all the gory details of the past two weeks.

"And she won't even give you a clue about who your real father is?" His eyebrows are so high they've disappeared under his hair.

"No!"

Gray Beard shoots us a look, and I giggle. Is he going to make us walk the plank? He's tending bar by himself now, and the place is really starting to fill up. Why hasn't Derek's replacement come?

"Well that sucks." Derek takes a sip of his own beer.

I watch his Adam's apple bob when he swallows. He has a looong neck. Like, sexy long. He flicks his hair out of his eyes, but it falls back down. I reach forward and brush is aside, running my fingers through the strands.

"You hair is sooo soft," I purr.

Even I notice how slurred the words are, but Derek just grins when I push my empty glass toward him. He leans over the bar and fills it back up.

"Thanks." I grab it. Liquid sloshes out and drips across my fingers. "I spilled. Want to lick it off?" I lift my hand toward him and smile in what I'm sure is a very sexy way. I *feel* sexy.

"I wouldn't want to take advantage." He wipes my hand off with a napkin and tosses it aside before pressing his lips to the top. "I should be a gentleman."

"How chivalrous of you." I pick my beer back up. "You have a white steed in the parking lot too?"

"Nope. But I have a red Mustang."

I laugh. "Well that's convenient."

Gray Beard comes over and clears his throat. "Dude. She ain't even legal."

Derek jumps to his feet. He leans over the bar and gets inches from Gray Beard's face. "Neither am I."

"Yeah," I yell. "Go back to your pirate ship!"

Derek laughs. He grabs my hand and pulls me to my feet. His skin is warm and smooth, and my fingers tingle when he laces his through mine. "I'll make sure she gets home."

Gray Beard glares at me. I close one eye and salute him. "Aye aye, captain!"

Derek laughs even louder, and I giggle. I take one quick drink before he pulls me toward the door. "Come on!" he says, pushing the door open.

When we step outside, cold air and snow flurries swirl around us. I shiver and cross my arms over my chest. Even alcohol can't keep a person warm tonight.

"Mike's gonna be pissed." Derek pulls out a pack of cigarettes, lights up, and blows smoke into the air. We watch it disappear between the falling snowflakes.

"Mike's the pirate you work for?"

The corner of his mouth pulls up. He takes another hit. "Yeah."

"No college?"

He flicks his cigarette and leans against the wall. I do the same, and the cold from the stone seeps through my clothes, coating my body in goose bumps. My cheeks are still warm from the alcohol, but every other inch of my body shivers. A jacket would have been smart.

"Naw. I'm still trying to figure out what to do with myself." He grins. "High school wasn't really my thing. Chemistry was the only class I ever looked forward to. And let me tell you, it had nothing to do with the subject."

His eyes move down my body. He's not checking me out, not in this baggy sweater and jeans. It's more like he's mentally undressing me. I rest my head against the building and let him.

"Did you have a thing for me, or did you just enjoy the thong?"

Derek laughs and the sound is so musical that I can almost imagine all the crap I've been through the last two weeks didn't really happen. "Oh yeah. I had it real bad."

I rock my head toward him. We're only a few inches apart. He exhales, and I can smell the beer and tobacco on his breath. His hair has fallen across his eyebrow again, and I reach up to brush it aside. He catches my hand in his before I can do it, but he doesn't say anything.

"And now?"

"I haven't seen you since that class. Not really."

"So that means you don't find me attractive?" I don't believe him. Not with the way his brown eyes search my face or the way he's holding my hand.

He swallows and flicks his cigarette to the ground. "You're drunk and you're hurting."

"I'm also wearing a thong."

He groans and looks up toward the sky, like he's asking God why. Snowflakes fall on his eyelashes, and he blinks. It all seems so surreal that I can't stop myself from reaching forward. I turn his face toward me, and before I can even register what's happening, his lips are on mine. He presses me against the building, his tongue dipping into my mouth. His hands move down my back, and he grabs my butt—actually grabs it! I moan and pull him closer, wrapping my arms around him and moving my hand down his back until I'm able to find my way under his jacket. When I touch bare skin, he sighs against my lips.

Bells ring and things heat up. Literally heat up. It takes me a few seconds to realize someone is standing next to us. Derek pulls his face away, but not his body. I'm still pressed against the building when I turn to face Gray Beard.

"What's up, Mike?" Derek says casually.

"Dude. You gotta get her outta here. If a cop comes we're screwed."

"We're outside."

Mike swears under his breath.

"Ease up," I say. "You look like your parrot died or something."

Mike scowls, but Derek laughs.

Derek grabs my hand and pulls me away from the building. "Okay, okay. We're going!" He's still laughing when I shiver. "You cold?" He puts his arm around my shoulders and pulls me against his lean body. "Come on. I'll keep you warm."

CHAPTER SIX

My eyes open to a *Star Wars* poster. I blink, but it's still there. When did I buy that?

My throat is scratchy and my mouth is dry, and it tastes like something curled up and died in it. When I try to sit up, my head pounds. Why did I drink so much? Oh yeah, my life sucks.

Someone grunts and the whole bed shifts when they move. My heart pounds, and even before I turn to see who it is, I remember. Derek. His eyes are still closed, and he's hugging his pillow. God, even in his sleep he looks sexy! But what the hell did I do? A one night stand? That isn't me. I've never done anything like this before!

Derek's eyelids flutter. They don't open, but I pull the sheet up to my chin anyway. I'm not wearing pants. I'm not wearing a shirt. I'm not wearing a *bra*. Oh…my…God!

Desperately, I scan the room in search of my clothes. My jeans are on top of a very unstable looking lamp, but I don't see my shirt or bra anywhere. Maybe I can somehow get this sheet off the bed and wrap it around me without waking Derek? It's worth a shot.

Very slowly, I pull the sheet toward me. It slides my

way a few inches then comes to an abrupt halt. I pull harder, but it doesn't budge. Then I yank it. Still nothing. What the hell? Is this thing stapled to the mattress or what?

I try one more time, and Derek's eyes fly open. He bolts upright, ripping the sheet right out of my hands. I'm naked except for a very skimpy thong. Then again, Derek is practically naked too. Black boxer briefs. That's it. His body is all lean wiry muscle. He's sexier than I would have imagined, and I feel a twinge of regret that I don't remember last night.

Derek blinks and rubs his eyes like a little kid. When his hands fall back to his side, he looks down at me and grins. "Morning, sunshine."

That snaps me out of it. I grab for the sheet and rip it away from him, pulling it back up to my chin. "Don't look!"

He stretches his arms above his head and the muscles in his shoulders and arms ripple. Then he drops his arms and plops back down next me. "Relax. I saw it all last night. You were very anxious to show me your thong."

I put my face in my hands. "I can't believe I did this!"

"What? Now that you're sober you don't find me as irresistible?"

Derek's voice is playful, but I can't relax. How could I have done something so stupid?

His fingers work their way behind my hands, and he gently pries them away from my face. "Kara, look at me."

I don't want to, but I force myself to meet his gaze. His brown eyes lock on mine, and then I remember. *That's* why I did something this stupid, because there's something about Derek that is just so…I don't even know. Amazing? Relaxing? Better than any drug?

"We didn't."

The words bounce around in my head, and I blink. "What?"

"You tried, believe me." He lets go of my hands and

throws himself back against his pillow. "I deserve a medal for last night," he says to the ceiling, "especially after that little dance you did."

I grip the sheet tighter, and my entire face bursts into flames. "I did a dance?" What's wrong with me?

He rolls over to face me, propping his head up with one arm. "I told you, you were very excited to show me your thong." I pull the sheet up over my face, but he immediately pulls it away. "But nothing else happened."

"Nothing?"

He shakes his head and grins. Oh, that grin! It makes my insides melt. "Not unless you count calling me a lot of very creative names for turning you down something."

"I did that?" I whisper. "I'm so sorry! Here you were trying to be a good guy, and I was mean to you."

"Don't sweat it. I enjoyed myself." His eyes move down, and every hair on my body stands up. It feels like he has X-ray vision. "Forget chemistry class. It had nothing on last night."

My cheeks burn even hotter, and he grins. How is it fair for a person to have such an amazing smile? No wonder I lost all control of my senses last night.

Derek rolls out of bed and walks across the room. I sit up for a better look, still clutching the sheet against my body. The muscles in his back ripple as he jerks the dresser drawer open. He isn't really muscular in the same way as Bill Harper, who's the only other guy I've seen this naked in person, but it's still hot. Bill wrestled and had an obsession with working out. His body was a rock, but not in a good way. Curling up with him on the couch wasn't comfortable. Then again, maybe that was his personality.

Derek pulls a shirt over his head, then tosses one my way. It hits me in the face, and when I accidentally drop the sheet, the corner of his mouth turns up. My cheeks burn, but this time I don't rush to cover up.

"Thanks," I say. He doesn't take his eyes off me while I pull it over my head. It's big enough that it will hang past my bare ass when I stand, so that helps me relax.

He's a total mute until my boobs are covered, but as soon as the shirt is over my head, he says, "Okay! What do you want? Coffee? Tylenol? Food?"

My stomach growls and my head pounds. "All three sound good."

"What about calling your mom?" I grimace, and he puts his hands up. "Fair enough. We'll worry about that later."

He heads to the door, and I jump off the bed. But I move too fast and have to stop when my ribs start to throb. I double over and clutch my side. Damn. Not completely healed yet.

Derek turns around with his hand on the doorknob, and his smile fades. "You alright?"

I nod. Nope. That wasn't a good idea. My brain feels like it's bouncing around inside my skull. "I'm alright, just moved a little too fast."

He comes over and puts his arm around me. "Let's get that Tylenol."

My hair is dripping when I step out of Derek's bathroom, but I'm dressed in my own clothes. Somehow I managed to find everything but a sock. I don't even want to think about the striptease I did that resulted in my clothes being strewn all over Derek's bedroom. How embarrassing.

"More coffee?" Derek is stretched out on the couch watching the Syfy channel. Some cheesy movie with a very unrealistic-looking giant crocodile. It stomps down the street crushing cars as three people fly above it in a helicopter, discussing their plan for stopping it.

I shake my head, and he scoots over so I can sit next to him. "What's this?"

I have the perfect view of his right cheek when the

dimple appears. "*Mega Python vs. Gatoroid.* It's a classic."

"I can see that." I stare at the screen for a few more minutes, but when my eyes glaze over I can't help it. The movie is beyond bad.

"You want to call your mom now?" Derek asks. "It's almost eleven."

"Let her sweat it out a little."

I can't focus on the movie, and my eyes wander the room. The walls are covered with family pictures. Derek and another boy a few years younger than him as children. The two smiling boys posing with their parents on the beach, by the Grand Canyon. At the zoo. It's cute.

He lives at home. I should freak out, but I don't. We've been up for almost three hours now; if his mom and dad were here we would have seen them by now. Maybe they're out of town?

I take a closer look at the pictures of his mom and dad. They seem happy. Derek looks a lot like his dad. "Where are your parents?"

"Dead." His voice is too even.

I turn to face him, but his eyes are focused on the TV. "Your brother?"

His jaw tightens, but his voice is just as level as it was before when he says, "Dead."

Suddenly, it all comes back to me. It happened senior year, just a few weeks before graduation. There was an accident. A car stalling on train tracks or something like that. Everyone heard about it, but I didn't know the kid who lost his whole family in the blink of an eye. That was Derek. It hasn't even been a year.

"I'm so sorry."

"Yeah. Me too." His jaw twitches and he starts flipping through the channels.

I'm such a jerk! I put my face in my hands. "All that drama I threw on you last night. It must have seemed like such a joke to you!"

He pulls my hands away. He's smiling, but it isn't as

light as it usually is. "No. You have a right to be upset. My family being killed doesn't have a thing to do with your mom lying to you."

"You're too nice." My throat is tight. Why is the world so shitty and how did I make it this far without knowing it? Have I been walking around in a bubble my whole life?

His brown eyes search mine and slowly his smile becomes sincerer. "Go out with me tonight."

My heart skips like a little girl playing hopscotch. What's with the mood swings? I'm just going to attribute it to Derek's Zoloft-ness. "You mean like a date?"

He grins and brushes the hair out of my face. "Yeah. Like a date."

Mom is on me the second I step into the house. "Kara! Where have you been?"

Her eyes are red and puffy, and she's wearing the same clothes as yesterday. It doesn't look like she's slept, and deep down I know I should feel bad for making her worry. I search every inch of myself, trying to find some sympathy. I come up empty.

"I went out."

"Out? You were gone all night. No car, no wallet—no jacket! I didn't know what happened to you. I called all the hospitals. The police. Where have you been all night?" I try to push past her, but she grabs my arm. "Kara!"

Her voice shakes. I exhale and fight down the anger. She's still my mom. No matter how angry I am with her, I have to work on fixing this. When I open my eyes, tears are falling down her cheeks, but I'm still empty inside.

"I ran into a friend from high school." Not a total lie. "So I crashed with them." There. The truth without revealing too much.

"You could have called!"

I jerk my arm out of her grasp and push past her. "Yes,

and you could have told me the truth about who I am. We don't always do the things we should." I trot up the stairs, calling over my shoulder, "I have a date tonight, too. If you want me to be able to call, you better work on getting me a replacement cell phone."

I slam my door and lean against it. My body shakes, but only part of it is from anger. The house feels even smaller than yesterday, and the constant tension is starting to get to me. But I can't make myself forgive her. I'm not ready yet. Dad is missing, and she still won't tell me anything about her past. Maybe if she could give just a little, I'd be able to, but she won't and it's so frustrating.

The clock flashes at me from the other side of the room like a beacon. It's already after two. Derek is supposed to pick me back up at five. My head pounds and I feel gross despite the shower and food I had at his place. Not the best night for a first date, but I have a feeling all the yuckiness will disappear the second I see him. There's just something about this guy…

The sound of the garage door opening makes me jump. I cross the room and get to the window just as Mom backs into the street. Three hours until I can get out of here. At least I don't have to deal with my mom the whole time, but what do I do until then?

My eyes land on the nightstand where I stashed the photo albums. Now would be a good time to look through them since there's no chance she'll walk in on me. I drop to my bed and wince when my ribs ache. It's bothering me more today than it was yesterday, I must have hurt them last night when I was drunk. Possibly during my striptease, which I still can't believe I did.

As soon as the pain subsides, I pull the albums out and start flipping through the first one. This time I go slow, studying each page carefully for any clues. A few of the photos are from a bowling league my parents were in. They all have matching blue shirts, and it looks like their last names are on the back. I look closer, but there isn't a clear shot of any of the names except the beginning of one. The Asian girl has her back to the camera in one of the pictures, and a few letters are visible. N-a-k-a. That has to tell me something.

I power up my laptop and drum my fingers on the desk while I wait for the virus scan to run. Taking notes would be a good idea. And not on the computer. I learned my lesson after the cell phone thing. Never again will I fail to write things down. I dig through the drawers in my desk and manage to find an old spiral notebook and a pen.

While I wait, I jot down the names I know: *Liz, Grace, Mark, Brad, Jeff,* and *Tobi Naka?* As soon as the computer is booted up, I open the Internet and Google Japanese surnames. I click on the first link. Now I'm getting somewhere! Right away my eyes land on Nakamura. Bingo! But then I scan the list some more and see Nakashima, followed by Nakagawa, Nakayama, and Nakano. Shit. How many Japanese names start with Naka?

I gnaw on my bottom lip while I jot them all down. What next? I could Google this chick with all these last names and see what comes up; it's not like Tobi is a common name. But it could be short for something. Plus, if she's gotten married it's possible nothing will come up at all. So I'm just as clueless as I was a few minutes ago! Crap.

I go back to the photo album and keep looking, but come up empty-handed, so I grab the second one and flip it open. The first few pictures have the group at a coffee shop. The redhead, Grace, is wearing an apron and carrying a tray. Her shirt says *Kent Coffee.* It's been a long time, but maybe it's a small enough place that they'd remember her? Probably not, but it wouldn't hurt to call and ask.

When I Google Kent Coffee I have the sudden urge to do a dance. They actually have a Website! It says, *family owned since 1970.* That's reassuring at least. There's a tab for pictures, so I click on it and keep my fingers crossed as it loads. Maybe they have pictures of old employees.

The first few are recent. A smiling girl with bright pink hair is wearing a shirt that says, *Bulldogs Class of 2013*. Luckily, there are captions with years under all the pictures, so I scroll down until I hit the late '90s. That's what I need. I was born in June of 1996, so Mom and Dad would have been hanging out with this group in 1995.

I scan the faces and in the third picture, I spot the redhead. She's standing with her arm around another girl, and they're both wearing Kent Coffee shirts. The caption under the picture says, *1996-Grace Abernathy and Julia Christian*.

Abernathy! My heart jumps and I jot the name down in my notebook before typing the name into Google. Of course, a million things pop up. A few links to Facebook pages, an obituary. The link to real estate page where the listing agent is named Grace Abernathy. I almost look right past it, but the word Kent jumps out at me and I squeal. Did I seriously find her that easily? No way!

I clink on the link, and her picture pops up. She's older, but it has to be her. Her red hair is wavy and hangs just past her shoulders, and her green eyes sparkle even in the picture. This is definitely the girl from the album, and she still lives in Kent!

I write down her phone number and the address for her office, but before I can do anything else the sound of the garage door opening fills the house. Crap! Mom's home. I shut the browser and shove the albums back into my nightstand, all while ripping off my clothes. The garage door shuts and I turn the shower on, hopping in before the water has even had a chance to get warm. It stings, and every inch of my body is covered in goose bumps within seconds, but by the time Mom walks through the door the bathroom is filled with steam.

"Your new phone is on your dresser!" she yells from the doorway. "Don't *ever* stay out all night without calling me again."

I salute her with my middle finger, which of course, she

doesn't see.

CHAPTER SEVEN

I clutch the damp towel tightly against my body, and I turn on my new phone. Twenty text messages. I scan the names as I flip through: Jess, Dee, Megan. They've texted me over and over again in the past two weeks. Why didn't any of them actually stop by the house?

But there's nothing from my dad. I exhale and close my eyes. He just needs time. After all, he did tell me I was still his daughter. The thought doesn't help relieve any of the tension in my body.

The time flashes across the screen. It's already after four, and I'm not even dressed! I need to get moving, but first I need to let the girls I haven't been abducted by aliens or fallen off the planet. I start a group text and quickly type. *Sorry I've been MIA. Had accident on the way home from school—my cell was toast. Just got a new one.*

After I hit send, I open a second text and type Dad's name in. What do I say? Do I tell him he's being a selfish jerk? Do I tell him I still need my dad? That I don't care about biology? No, I can't do that. If he doesn't answer it would hurt too much. Instead, I type, *Hoping 2 hear from U. Love U.*

Now I can focus on getting ready for my date.

I'm in the middle of blow drying my hair when my phone explodes. Without turning the dryer off, I pick it up and scroll through the messages.

Jess: *OMG!! R U OK??*

Dee: *Accident? Like a car accident?*

Megan: *I thought you were out of town!! I'm such a jerk!*

Still nothing from Dad. I try not to think about it while I type my reply.

Kara: *Wasn't a big deal. Totaled the car, but I just had a few bruised ribs and spleen. Been trapped at the house. U won't believe what's been going on.*

I go back to drying my hair, but it's less than thirty seconds before my phone starts going off again. Crap. At this rate, I'm never going to be ready on time.

I turn the blow dryer off and sit on the floor.

Megan: *Grab your shoes I'm coming 2 get U!*

Dee: *That blows. U get a new car?*

Jess: *OMG!*

Kara: *Thanx Meg, but I have a date—long story. Maybe tomorrow we can meet up?*

Megan: *Heading back 2 school in the AM*

Crap.

Jess: *Date? With who!?! :-o*

Dee: *Going back 2 school 2. Who R U going out with?*

Kara: *Damn. I really wanted to see U girlz. You going back 2 Jess? Derek Miller. Do U remember him?*

Jess: *Yup. The nerdy computer guy from HS?*

Dee: *From HS? How did that happen?*

Megan: *Didn't his family die senior year?*

Nerdy? There's nothing about Derek that struck me as particularly nerdy. Well, maybe the *Star Wars* poster, but lots of people love *Star Wars*; that doesn't mean anything. But there was also that Syfy movie he was watching…

I pull myself to my feet and head back into my bedroom. My yearbook is next to the computer. I flip it open and scan the pictures of the senior class until I find

Derek. "OMG" is right! He doesn't look anything like the guy I met last night. No wonder I didn't remember him. He has thick glasses and braces, and his hair is way too short. This guy I vaguely remember, although not from chemistry class. What a difference a year makes.

I toss the book aside and pick my phone back up. Dee and Jess have already texted me again.

Dee: *Oh yeah! I remember him.*

Jess: *Weird.*

Kara: *Just looked up his picture—he does not look like that anymore! Meg—yes, that was him.*

Megan: *Well that sucks.*

Dee: *He's hot now?*

Jess: *Nice ass?*

I snort and cover my mouth again. I've missed these girls so much!

Kara: *Seeexy.*

I press my lips together. Should I do it? It will drive them mad not knowing the story. Yeah, I can't resist.

Kara: *Woke up naked in his bed this morning ;-)*

I hold my breath and count. One, two, three—my phone blows up.

Dee: *What????? U have 2 tell!*

Jess: *Slut!*

Megan: *Seriously, that is SO not like you! Was it good?*

I giggle, but before I can respond another text pops up.

Jess: *Where R U guys going tonight? We could "accidentally" pop by! ;-p*

Actually, I have no idea, but that doesn't sound like a bad idea. I'd get to see the girls, fill them in on what's been happening, *and* show off Derek.

Kara: *Don't know yet. When he picks me up, I'll text U. Gotta get ready though!*

Crap. It's a quarter till. He'll be here soon!

Jess: *U better!*

Dee: *B there! I promise not to steal him ;-)*

Megan: *What if it scares him off?*

I roll my eyes and toss my phone on the bed. Megan—she always has to be the responsible one. Of course, I shouldn't complain. She's kept us out of trouble on more than one occasion.

I get ready in record time, and when I open my bedroom door Mom's voice floats up from downstairs. Is Derek here already? Talking to *her*? Why didn't she come get me?

I charge down the stairs, ignoring the pain in my ribs and side, and dash into the living room. Derek is sitting on the couch and he grins when I walk in. Immediately, every muscle in my body melts like butter in a hot skillet. He looks amazing! Chocolate brown leather jacket, dark-blue shirt that hugs his chest just right. I have no idea where we're going for dinner, but I know what I'm having for dessert.

"Kara," Mom says with a huge smile on her face. "Derek was just telling me about last night." My mouth drops open, but Mom doesn't seem to notice. She gets to her feet and smiles at Derek like he's some kind of hero. "What a gentleman you found!"

Derek snickers. What did he tell her? Not the real story. That would be nuts!

"Yeees," I say, stretching out the word as long as possible, hoping it distracts her from asking me anything else.

Mom can't take her eyes off Derek. "It was so nice of him to give you a ride to Megan's house. I'm sure she was happy to hear from you."

I raise an eyebrow, but Derek just keeps grinning. "Yes, it *was* nice of him."

"Well, it was really nice to meet you, Mrs. Jones," Derek says, jumping to his feet and crossing the room to me in two long strides. "We better be heading out though."

"Okay!" Mom sings. "Have a good time!"

The second the door is closed behind us, I turn to

Derek. "What did you tell her?"

He grabs my hand and pulls me toward the car. "I just told her that I saw you walking on the side of the road and recognized you, so I picked you up and gave you a lift to Megan's house. She's the only one of your friend's names I could remember. Luckily, you're still friends with her, and your mom didn't think it was weird."

He stops outside the passenger door, and I have to bend my head way back to meet his gaze. He's nearly a full head taller than me. "You should have seen the look on your face." The little dimple in his right cheek winks at me.

"I'm glad I amuse you." I try to sound annoyed, but it doesn't work. I'm not. Just like last night, his relaxed attitude has a calming effect on me.

A cold breeze catches my hair, blowing it across my face. Derek tucks it behind my ear, then runs his fingertips down the side of my cheek to my jaw. Then up to my lips. He traces the bottom one with his thumb, and the temperature outside goes up about a hundred degrees.

"Can I kiss you?"

A nervous laugh pops out of my throat. "Now?"

Derek leans closer. His warm breath caresses my skin. It smells like cinnamon and feels like silk. "Yeah. Last night, you were drunk."

"But you weren't."

His hand runs down my arm, and my skin tingles. "No, but I want you coherent."

He *wants* me. That's all I can focus on when I nod. He grasps my chin and tilts my face up toward his, and when his lips touch mine, my eyes close on their own. His mouth is soft and warm. Gentle. It isn't urgent like last night when he pressed me against the wall, it's sweet. Just like him. He laughs against my lips, and I open my eyes, pulling back so I can see him. His big brown eyes are dancing. Where did this guy come from?

"I never thought I'd get to kiss Kara Jones." There he goes again, caressing my name with his tongue. Making my body jealous.

My legs tremble, but luckily, my voice comes out even. "You say it like I'm something amazing."

His hand is still on my face, and he brushes his thumb against my lips again. "You are. I don't know how you don't know that." He exhales and takes a step back. "Okay. Date time."

I giggle. I can't help it. He makes me giddy. "So where are we going?"

He stuffs his hands in the pockets of his leather jacket. "No idea. Dinner? It's early, but I figured you'd want to get out of the house as soon as possible. Are you hungry now?"

"I could eat. What did you have in mind?" I have to text the girls. There is no way they are going back to school without meeting Derek!

"Lady's choice."

"You know what really sounds good? Marion's."

He pulls the passenger door open, sweeping his arm gallantly toward the car. "Pizza it is then."

It's Saturday night, so Marion's is packed, as usual. I inhale when we walk through the door, and my entire body is suddenly lighter. It isn't just the pizza—even though it *is* the best pizza in the world—it's this place. It feels like home. The brown tiled floors and dark atmosphere, the brick walls and iron dividers that surround the dining areas. The murals painted on the back wall. It's all part of my childhood. I've been here hundreds of times over the years, with parents and friends, boyfriends and first dates.

"So what do you like?" Derek slings his arm across my shoulders and casually plays with my hair. It makes me shiver.

"Pepperoni and black olives?" I peer at him through my hair while keeping one eye on the door. Megan, Jess, and Dee should be waltzing in anytime now.

He pulls me toward the back of the line. "Sounds good."

I chew on my fingernail while we wait to order. Did I make a mistake inviting the girls here? Megan thinks it will scare Derek off, but I don't think so. I glance at him out of the corner of my eye, but he seems totally relaxed. He picks up one of the packages of gummy bears, studies it for a second, then sets it aside. Gummy worms apparently are better, because he keeps those. I have to agree.

There are more than a few familiar faces in the crowd tonight and my stomach is suddenly unstable. I hadn't thought about running into anyone I knew other than the girls. What will I say if someone asks about my family? I can't talk about it.

Derek leans down, so his face is next to mine. "You okay?"

"What am I supposed to say to people if they ask how I've been?"

He gives my hand a quick squeeze. "Just say fine and turn it back around on them."

He's right. There's no law that says I have to tell anyone what's been going on. Let Mom do the explaining. She can figure out what to tell people when they split up.

My stomach twists even more. Are my parents headed for divorce? All these years I've counted myself lucky. I'm one of the few people I know whose parents are still married. My friends all have parents and stepparents to worry about, not to mention the endless string of dates some of the less grown-up parents bring home. My life has always been easy. Mom and Dad and me. What's it going to be like now?

"Kara!"

I jump at the sound of my name and spin around to face the girls. They're standing at the back of the line grinning at me like idiots. Dee's gray eyes are about to pop out of her head as she stares at Derek. She pats her brown curls in place before flashing him a brilliant smile. She's such a flirt!

"Hi!" I squeak.

"It's so crazy running into you here!" Jess flips her blonde hair over her shoulder and bats her eyes at Derek. I cringe. She isn't the least bit convincing.

Derek clears his throat, but before I can say anything, it's his turn to order. He winks at me, then turns to the cash register.

Dee grabs my arm and pulls me toward them. "OMG!" she hisses. "That cannot be Derek Miller!"

"Shhh!" I glance over my shoulder at Derek, but he still has his back to me, thank God. "Will you just chill!"

"So you guys did it?" Jess asks. Too loud.

Everyone in line turns to look at us, including Derek. He heads our way with a giant grin on his face and my cheeks get hotter than a volcano before it erupts.

He puts his hand on my lower back before turning to the girls. "So I take it you ladies will be joining us?"

Megan—the saint—shakes her head and narrows her green eyes at Jess and Dee. "We wouldn't want to get in the way."

Dee shoots her a dirty look just as Jess says, "But it would be nice to catch up!"

Derek just grins. "It's no big deal. Go ahead and order while Kara and I find a table."

My armpits are sweating, but Derek is all smoothness as he leads me through the restaurant.

"So you got a new phone today?" I start to protest, but he chuckles. "Don't worry, I get it. You wanted to show off your prize."

My mouth drops open. Can he read my mind?

He elbows me lightly. "I'm kidding, Kara."

Oh, thank God. I laugh, but it's shaky. "They're all going back to school tomorrow morning, and I wanted to see them before they left."

"You could have just told me."

Kate L. Mary

"I didn't want to upset you." I give him the shakiest smile in the history of the world.

He rolls his eyes and pulls a chair out for me. "Did you even hear what I said outside your house? I probably should play hard to get, but I think it's a little too late for that."

I take a seat and in one swift move, he lowers himself into a chair, puts the receipt on the table, and holds out his hand. "Let me see your phone."

"My phone?"

He waves his fingers at me. What could it hurt?

I hand it over and he chuckles as he types something in. His phone number maybe? I don't have it, so that would makes sense.

"All done." He plops it in front of me and crosses his arms over his chest.

"You look awfully proud of yourself," I say, pulling up the contacts. When Derek's name pops up, I roll my eyes. "'Derek "the-sex-god" Miller.' Really?"

"That's what your friends seem to think. Not sure what you might have said to give them that impression," he says with a wink.

I roll my eyes again, but my cheeks are on fire. I can't believe he heard that.

Before I can say anything else, Jess pulls out the chair next to me. Her brown eyes dance and she's so excited that she's shaking like a Chihuahua. "Exactly how did this happen?"

60

CHAPTER EIGHT

"Was it awful?"

The girls just left, and Derek is finishing off the last of their pizza. He seemed alright with the whole thing, but Dee and Jess can be a lot to take sometimes. Thank God for Megan! I'm going to have to send her flowers or something for being so amazing. She saved me from more than one humiliating moment.

"Your friends are nice," he says with his mouth full.

"All their questions weren't annoying?"

He swallows and grins, and his dimple is deeper than ever. "Actually, it was pretty amusing. Seeing how red your face got every time Jess asked something awkward made the whole thing worthwhile."

"What about Dee?"

"What about her?"

"Derek! She was flirting with you the whole time."

"No she wasn't." He waves his hand in the air and goes back for more pizza.

"Um, yes she was."

My phone dings and I pull up the text.

Dee: *Yummy. Soooo pissed U saw him first!*

I shove the phone toward Derek. "Told you!"

The corner of Derek's mouth turns down, and he shakes his head. "I'm not that different from high school."

"Please!" His frown deepens, and I roll my eyes yet again. If I'm not careful, they're going to get stuck that way. "Whatever."

Derek swallows the last bite of pizza and leans back, patting his stomach like it's huge. It isn't. I could wash clothes on it. If this was 1890.

"So what do you want to do now?" he asks.

"Not go home."

His eyebrows pull together and I immediately regret saying it. Way to ruin the light mood! "Forget I said it. Let's go to a movie or something."

He takes my hand and rubs his thumb across the top in small circles. "No. Talk about it. You can't just shove it all inside."

I watch his thumb move, making invisible rings on my hand. What would I do right now if I hadn't met him? He saved me last night. I was about to lose my mind, and if he hadn't been in that pool hall, I would have just had to turn around and go back to my mom. With my tail tucked between my legs. And now? How many guys would be this understanding? None.

"I just…" I close my eyes, and when I open them all I can see are his eyes staring back at me. "I want to know where I come from."

"Your mom still won't budge?"

"No. And she's not going to change her mind. I know her. Once she makes a decision, she doesn't back down. I just don't get how she can't understand why I need to know."

Derek stops rubbing my hand and sits back. "So what do you know so far?"

"What do you mean?"

"Well, you have to know something that might help you figure out who your father is on your own."

I throw my hands in the air. "I wish! All I really know is my mom was going to grad school at Kent State when she got pregnant with me, and my dad was teaching at the local high school. I've never heard a single story about someone they were friends with or anything they ever did when they lived there. It never seemed strange to me before, but now it's obvious why!"

I exhale, and Derek scoots his chair closer. He rubs my back, but it doesn't help. My insides are wound so tight that I feel like I'm wearing a corset.

"Relax," Derek says. "We'll figure it out."

Is this guy for real? "We?" My voice sounds so small.

That dimple gets deeper. "Yeah."

My throat tightens, and I have to swallow before I can say anything. "Derek…"

He squeezes my hand, then starts chewing on his lip. "There has to be something else."

"I found a photo album."

He leans closer. "Go on."

I tell him all about the coffee shop and my mom's friends, how I found Grace's Web site and half of Tobi's last name. He listens without interruption, chewing on his bottom lip the whole time, which I have to admit I find incredibly sexy.

"Well, we can call Grace's office tomorrow during business hours. And as far as this Tobi woman goes, you have half a last name. I bet there's an alumni page or something. We could start there."

My jaw drops. Why didn't I think of that? "You're a genius!" Without thinking, I lean forward and kiss him. Right on the mouth, right in the middle of the restaurant.

Derek's eyebrows shoot up. He leans back and crosses his arm over his chest. I have no idea what he's thinking. Is he just surprised? It's hard to tell; his expression is so blank.

Finally, after what seems like days, he clears his throat. "What are you going to do if we find this Tobi woman?

Take off your clothes?" His lips twitch. "Oh wait! You already did that."

I laugh and shake my head, and Derek jumps to his feet.

"What are you doing?" The words are shaky thanks to the laughter rolling through me. There's still a slight ache in my chest from my injuries, but it feels good to have something to joke about.

Derek grabs my hand and hauls me to my feet. "You want to find this Tobi lady, right?" I nod. "No time like the present then. Let's head back to my place and do some searching. You can find anything on the Internet."

Derek stops in the middle of unlocking his front door and turns to face me. "Now, if I let you into my house you have to promise not to attack me."

The wind howls. I shiver. "Right now I'm so cold that the only thing I want to attack is a cup of coffee."

Derek laughs and pushes the door open. God I love his laugh. Is it possible it's only been a little over twenty-four hours since I met him? I'm so comfortable around him already.

I stomp on the welcome mat to knock the snow off my boots before I step inside. The house is warm and inviting, like crawling into a freshly made bed. Or like coming home. Not my home, of course.

Derek tosses his coat on a chair and flips the light on. "I'll get my laptop. Get comfortable."

He goes into the other room, and I flop onto the couch. It smells like Derek, and the pit of my stomach starts to tingle when I think about this morning. Waking up in his bed. Naked. What a gentleman he was. How sexy he looked…

"Okay!"

I jump when he walks back into the room.

He plops down next to me and balances the laptop on his knees. It looks tiny sitting on his long legs. "Kent State alumni," he says, typing.

I have to bite back a smile because it reminds me of someone moving their lips when they read, and for some odd reason it makes me want to attack him. What's wrong with me? Sex has never really been on my list of priorities, especially not after Bill. It's not like he did anything to make the experience memorable.

"Here we go!" The link for the Kent State University Alumni Association pops up.

"Holy crap! No way it's going to be this easy."

"But we can't search without creating an account."

"So we just make a fake one."

He clicks on *first-time login*, and I hold my breath while the page loads. I have to resist the urge to squeal with excitement when it's done. There's a box in the middle of the page where you can type in the last name of the alumni.

"Meyer! Her maiden name was Meyer!" I practically yell.

Derek jerks his head away from me but grins anyway. He types Meyer, and about three hundred names come up. I scan the names while he scrolls down, pointing when I spot my mom.

"There! Charlotte, that's my mom!" But when the next page loads my heart sinks. "What's a Kent State constituent ID number?"

We both read the screen, and Derek's eyebrows pull together. "Do your parents get the Kent State magazine?"

I lean against the back of the couch. "Not that I know of."

Derek puts the computer on the table and pulls me against him. "We'll figure it out. None of this will really matter if we can get in touch with Grace Abernathy tomorrow. Right?"

He's right. So what if I can't make a fake profile and

join the alumni page? Grace Abernathy will know Tobi's last name. Hell, she may even know where Tobi lives now, and if she's married. They could be next door neighbors.

I turn my head toward Derek and bury my face in his chest. He smells good. I'm not sure what it is, but it reminds me of camping. Outdoorsy. I inhale and let the scent move through my body. It's more relaxing than smoking pot.

"Thank you."

He kisses my forehead, and it's like a lightning bolt shoots through my body, starting at my head and moving down. I move my face up to his neck and breathe in more of him. What's wrong with me? This is so not like me. I've been like the Ice Queen since Bill.

"Kara."

"Hmm." I can't seem to form actual words.

"Maybe this isn't such a good idea."

I pull back and look up at him. For the first time there's uncertainty in his eyes. "What are you talking about?"

He detaches himself from my arms and stands up. "I really like you."

"I like you, too."

He shakes his head. "No. I mean, I *really* like you. When I came up to take your order last night, I was playing dumb, acting like I didn't recognize you. I knew exactly who you were."

"Okay…" I still don't know where he's going with this. Didn't I just say I liked him too?

He swears and turns away. I don't know what to say to him. Does he think I'm using him? He must. How much of a bitch was I in high school?

I pull myself up and go over to him, putting my hands on his shoulders. "Derek, I like you too. For real."

He turns around, and my arms drop to my sides. "I've had a pretty crappy year."

My hand flies to my mouth. I've been *so* selfish. All I've

talked about the past twenty-four hours are my stupid problems. He lost his entire family. "Oh Derek, I'm so sorry."

He takes a step back. "I didn't say that so you'd feel bad for me. I just need you to know."

"I'm sorry. I'm so, *so* sorry! We can just forget my stupid crap. From here on out we won't talk about it."

The corner of his mouth turns up. "That's not what I meant. Kara…"

I shiver. There's that caress again. Why do I get the chills every time he says my name?

He swipes his hand through his hair and slowly exhales. "Your problems are not trivial. I may have lost my family, but I can still sympathize with what you're going through."

My eyes fill with tears, and before I can stop it a sob breaks out of my throat, shaking my entire body. Derek pulls me against him.

"I'm sorry," he whispers against my head. "I didn't mean to make you think that. I just wanted you to know that this is real for me."

I pull back. "What was I like in high school? Was I mean to you?"

He brushes a tear off my cheek. "You think I'd have it this bad if you'd been mean? You were nice to me, Kara. You may not really remember me, but you were always sweet."

How can I not remember him? I mean, I do, but only in passing. I have no recollection of him being in any of my classes. But chemistry was only two years ago.

"You said hi to me every morning and whenever you caught me staring—which was a lot—you smiled. You didn't make me feel bad for thinking you were pretty. You didn't act like I wasn't good enough for you. You treated me like a person. That was the most I could have hoped for back then."

"I wish I'd taken the time to get to know you." We weren't exactly in the same social circles, but I don't want to say that.

He leads me to the couch. When he sinks down he pulls me onto his lap, and I suddenly feel very small. "I don't want to overstep here, but things changed at the end of the year. I got the impression that you were going through a lot."

Bill. He's one of my greatest regrets. "Things didn't end well with Bill."

"I figured. You were different after the two of you broke up."

"He was such an ass." I don't want to tell him, but the words come out before I can stop them. "Our entire relationship was him pressuring me. All he wanted was sex. I know that now. At the time, I was too in love with the idea of him to really understand. He made me feel bad whenever I said no, like I was being mean to him. Even when I finally gave in things didn't get better."

Derek is frozen in place, and when I turn to look at him his eyes are like steel.

"Does this bother you?" I don't know what the etiquette is for talking about past partners; Bill's the only person I've ever been with. After that experience, I can't really say I've been anxious to jump back into a sexual relationship.

"A little, but it shouldn't. It isn't like I'm a virgin."

"Really?" I have to ask, I can't help it. It seems unfair that he'd know who I slept with, but I know nothing about him. "Do tell."

Derek looks away. "It's nothing to brag about, and with you sitting here it kind of makes me feel like a jerk."

I snort, which I realize the second I've done it that it's very unbecoming. "I can't imagine you doing anything that would make you an ass. Since I walked into that pool hall last night you've been nothing but honorable."

He clears his throat and stares at the ceiling. "That isn't exactly true."

"What do you mean?" He won't look at me, so I grab

his chin and turn his face toward me. "I danced naked for you last night, and you didn't do a thing! Right?" If I find out now that he lied after putting him up on a pedestal all day, I'm going to punch him in the balls.

His eyes dart to the side a few times. He won't meet my gaze. "Well…the striptease *may* have been my idea."

"Derek!" I shove him, but it's halfhearted, and when his eyes finally meet mine, they're sparkling. Oh, he feels *really* bad. Although, for some reason the fact that he doesn't feel bad makes my insides warm and tingly.

"Okay," I say, "now you really have to tell me. I need to know if you're a jerk or not. Talking a drunk girl into stripping for you is not very encouraging."

He grimaces and looks down at his hands. "You remember Becky Hines?"

"The head cheerleader?" Did he sleep with *her*? I try to keep my face expressionless, so he can't see my disgust. It isn't easy.

"Yeah. Well, a few months ago she came in with some friends. She didn't recognize me, and I wasn't about to tell her who I was. I don't know what she was like with you in high school, but to me she was—"

"Queen Bitch?"

He grins and looks up, but now I wish he'd go back to staring at his hands. If he slept with Becky Hines, I'm going to be sick.

"Yeah. Anyway, she was really flirting with me, but there was no way that was happening." Thank God! "So I started flirting with her friend. I didn't really mean for anything to happen, but she came back in the next night, and we went out…" He shrugs and all my insides relax. That's not so bad.

"It's not like you did it to get back at Becky, right?"

"No, but afterward I sure was hoping her friend would tell Becky all about it."

I don't miss the fact he hasn't mentioned the friend's name. Did she go to high school with us too? Do I want to know? Derek grabs a few strands of my hair and twists them around his fingers, and when his knuckles brush against my cheek my insides shudder. No, I do not want to know who it was.

"Okay, that's not such a big deal. Was that it then?"

"High school girlfriend. Senior year, after prom."

Since I don't remember him in high school, I don't know who his girlfriend was. Of course, it's also possible that even if he said her name, I wouldn't know who she was. It was a big school.

"My parents and brother had died a month before, and I only went to the prom because I needed something normal in my life for a night. I think she did it because she felt bad for me." He shrugs and the desire to wrap my arms around him is so overwhelming I have a hard time holding back. I lace my fingers through each other and put them in my lap. "We went out for a few more months after that, but we broke up right before she went off to college."

He stops twisting my hair. "Now you know," he says with a shrug. "You?"

"Just Bill."

His eyebrows shoot up. "That's it? But that was almost two years ago."

"So?"

"But—It's just—" He frowns and finally says, "You're hot."

Warmth spreads through my entire body and I can't ignore the twinge of desire rumbling in my stomach and lower. But I laugh his words off so he doesn't know. "I didn't say I *couldn't* have had sex in the last two years, just that I didn't."

He squirms underneath me and clears his throat. Why is he suddenly uncomfortable? Maybe I'm hurting him? I roll off his lap and inhale sharply when I turn wrong and pain shoots through my ribs. My hands go to my side just as Derek reaches for me. Somehow I end up knocking his hands away from their original target, and they end up right on my left boob.

He jerks them back like they've been burned and his face turns bright red, but he's smiling. "Sorry. That wasn't what I was going for."

My whole body is on fire, but I play it off. "Sure. I bet you've been planning that since we got here."

He clears his throat. "Anyway… So we're going to give this Grace chick a call tomorrow. What else do you have planned?"

Does he think I was serious? "Derek, I was *joking.*"

"I know, but it's not like I can really deny it."

My mouth drops open and he shrugs, but he doesn't look apologetic.

His mouth twitches like he's trying to hold in a smile. "Every time you touch me I can't help thinking about ripping your clothes off."

Oh my God! My insides are on fire. "Funny, I've had the same thing on my mind."

He blinks and I hold my breath, waiting for him to make a move. To kiss me or something. But nothing happens, and the silence stretches out between us until he finally jumps up and takes a few steps away. My heart sinks. He isn't going to kiss me?

"Okay. So first we call this Grace chick. Once we have some more information we can try using the Internet to look up these other people. One of them has to know something." He paces the room, not looking at me.

Boy, I feel like a jerk. "That sounds good."

He nods and leans against the wall. It's the furthest he can be from me without being in a different room.

"What's the deal, Derek?"

"I don't want to take advantage."

"Advantage! Seriously? How can you say that?"

"Because you're going through a difficult time. Obviously, sex isn't something you take lightly. I mean, two years…that's a long time."

I guess I shouldn't have told him that. "You wouldn't be taking advantage."

"I'd rather wait. It would make me feel better."

I throw myself against the back of the couch. "Fine."

"I'm sorry."

"You don't have to be sorry." I shake my head and sit up. "Do I have to go home, though? If I promise to be a good girl, will you let me stay the night again?"

His lips twitch. "As long as you promise."

Damn. I was hoping he'd let me be very, very bad.

CHAPTER NINE

I wake to the buzzing of my phone as it vibrates against the nightstand. Derek groans and rolls away from me, and I slam my hand against the table, feeling around for it. When my fingers finally wrap around my phone, I open one eye. A text from my mom. Crap. I should have sent her a message last night.

Mom: *If you don't text me back right away I'm calling the police.*

Double crap.

Kara: *I'm OK. Fell asleep watching a movie—on Derek's couch. Just woke up.*

Mom: *It is NOT acceptable to sleep over at a guy's house!*

Seriously? She's telling me what isn't acceptable? It's too early to fight, so I turn the phone off and put it back on the table.

When I roll over, Derek is staring at me. He grins. "Morning."

"Morning."

"Mom issues?"

He stretches, and the movement pulls the sheet down. Just like yesterday I'm wearing only a thong. Derek tried to talk me into putting one of his shirts on—part of that good girl thing—but I can't sleep in clothes. They get all twisted and it drives me nuts.

"I should have texted her last night." I shrug. Whatever.

Derek inhales sharply. He's staring at my bare chest and that same desire I felt last night swirls in my belly, moving lower until I seriously consider breaking my promise to be good.

But he's focused on my injuries. He reaches over and runs his fingers between my breasts. My eyes follow their progress as he traces his way down over my bruises, now more yellow than purple, before moving under my left boob and down my side. He stops just above my hip bone, and I have to clench my fists to keep from pushing him onto his back. When he starts tracing his way back up my body, my heart rate picks up. He moves his hand up my side then over, barely grazing the bottom of my breast when he passes under it. Then back up the center of my body, over the little dip between my collar bones and up my neck. From there he runs the back of his hand across my cheek and I shiver.

"You cold?"

I shake my head, and he grins. His thumb takes over where his hand left off, and he traces my lips. If only he'd stop teasing me. Or tease me more. I'm not even sure what I want.

He drops his hand and rolls over with a groan, throwing his legs over the side of the bed. He adjusts himself—that almost does me in—and turns his back to me. "Grace Abernathy should be in the office about now. It's almost nine."

I exhale, and he looks over his shoulder while he pulls a pair of plaid pajama pants on. He's grinning.

"Right. Grace Abernathy." I'm having a difficult time focusing, so I have no idea how he's able to think clearly. It's not like any blood is going to his brain right now.

He tosses me the same shirt I wore yesterday, and I pull it over my head.

"Sorry," he says, "the bruises distracted me." He grins. "I meant to say something about them yesterday, but I was too busy trying to convince you that you hadn't turned into a total slut."

I'm suddenly in a crappy mood. Probably has something to do with Derek being such a tease. "I need coffee," I grumble.

My hand shakes as I put the phone to my ear. What am I supposed to say to this woman? She's going to think I'm insane if I tell her the truth, but if I don't I won't be able to get any answers out of her.

"Maybe this is a stupid idea," I say to Derek, just as someone picks up.

"Abernathy Reality, this is Jean."

Crap. Well it's too late now. "Is Grace Abernathy in?"

"She sure is, can I tell her who's calling?"

A crazy person in search of the truth. "My name is Kara Jones."

There's a shuffling sound on the other end, and Jean says, "Please hold."

Taking her advice, I hold my breath.

"This is Grace," comes a crisp, professional voice.

Here goes nothing. "Um, hi. My name is Kara Jones and I'm the daughter of Greg and Charlotte Jones—I think you went to college with my mom."

There's a pause where my heart starts beating even faster. Maybe this *isn't* the right Grace Abernathy?

"Of course!" Grace's voice becomes less professional, and she laughs like she's talking to an old friend. "It took me a few seconds. It's been a long time. How are your parents?"

Now what do I say? They're fighting because we just

found out what a whore my mom was? "They're okay." I just need to put it out there. "This is going to sound really strange, but I was wondering if you had any idea who my real father is?"

A longer pause. I glance at Derek, who is sitting across from me at the kitchen table. His coffee mug is halfway to his mouth, and his eyes are huge. Crap. Maybe I shouldn't have said it like that.

Grace coughs. "I'm sorry?"

"No, I'm sorry. I know this is awkward, but I had to give it a shot and this is the only way I know how. I recently found out that my dad—Greg Jones—isn't actually my biological father. My dad had no idea, and my mom refuses to tell me anything about who my real father is. Contacting people who knew her back then was the only thing I could think to do. Do you have any idea who my mom may have cheated on my dad with?"

"Umm…" There's a shuffling sound and talking in the background, and Grace's voice is suddenly muffled like she's pulled the phone away from her face. I hear her telling someone that she needs a few minutes, and then she's back. "I'm really sorry, but I have no idea."

I exhale. "Okay. I'm sorry to bother you."

"No, no. Don't be." Grace sighs, and I can picture her shaking her head, her red hair bouncing around her shoulders. "Listen, I was really more friends with your dad than your mom. She was…well, she went through a tough time. They broke up for a few weeks. Did you know that?"

"Yes. I guess that's when my real father came into the picture."

"She was different after that. Nervous all the time. I don't know… Maybe someone else knows something?"

"Well, that's the problem. There's no one else for me to ask. I found a photo album with some pictures in it, but I only have first names. I came across your name accidentally and thought I'd give it a shot."

"What names did you find?"

I wish I had my notebook! "You, Liz, Tobi—and I have half of her last name—Mark, Brad and Jeff."

"That's easy enough. Liz's last name was Marcum, but she got married. Her married name was…" Grace clicks her tongue a few times. "Winston! Not sure if they're still together, but you can try both."

I snap my fingers at Derek and mouth *pen and paper*. He's still frozen, but he recovers quickly and scrambles to the kitchen. Thankfully, there's a pad of paper and a pen lying on the counter.

He slides them in front of me, and I balance the phone between my cheek and shoulder. "Okay. Liz Marcum or Winston," I say while I jot the names down.

"Yeah. And Tobi's last name was Nakamura. I doubt it's changed—I'm pretty sure she was a lesbian. Last I heard she lived in Detroit." There's a tapping sound on the other end of the line like Grace is drumming her fingers on the desk. "Mark Hilton—he actually still lives in Kent. I run into him from time to time. Brad Roth. I have no idea what happened to him. Then there's Jeff Hayes." She stops talking, and I hold my breath. "He's my ex-husband, and if he's your father, I'm going to cut his balls off. He still lives here in Kent too."

My heart is pounding and I'm writing a million miles a minute, but the smile on my face is so big my cheeks hurt. "Thanks! You have no idea how much this means to me!"

"I just wish I had more information for you." She pauses then snaps her fingers. "Try Kelly Duncan. Not sure if she ever got married, but she was your mom's roommate, and she may know something. I'm not sure how close they were. Kelly didn't come around much—she had her own boyfriend. I can't remember his name. Maybe someone else will."

"Thanks!"

"No problem. What's your e-mail? If I think of anything else I can shoot you a message."

I give her my e-mail address and thank her about thirty

more times before finally hanging up. All I can do is stare at the piece of paper in front of me. I went from nothing to a whole list of possibilities!

Derek already has his laptop open, and he's typing in the first name, Liz Marcum. I hold my breath, but nothing much comes up. A couple profiles on LinkedIn, neither of which could be her, and another on Facebook. The girl looks like she's thirteen.

"Try Winston."

That brings up a dozen possibilities, and Derek and I spend the next few hours scrolling through pages, searching through profiles and writing down possible phone numbers and addresses. We come up with the addresses for Mark and Jeff easily since they still live in Kent, and Tobi Nakamura, it turns out, lives in Cleveland. The others are more difficult. We uncover a few suspects, but nothing confirmed yet.

By one o'clock, my neck is sore, my stomach is growling, and my mom has texted me about thirty times. I've answered her once.

"Your mom is going to have a heart attack if you don't go home soon."

I lean against the chair, rubbing the back of my neck. Derek pushes my hand away and takes over. The second his fingers dip down the back of my shirt desire starts swirling around in the pit of my stomach again. He brushes the hair off my neck and massages my sore muscles with the same hands that moved down my body a few hours ago.

"I have to go to work soon." He's so close his breath tickles my skin, making the hair on my neck stand up.

"I guess I should go home and face my mom." I don't want to, and not just because of my mom. Being with Derek is so relaxing. I want to hide out in his house and pretend everything else didn't really happen.

Neither one of us moves. He keeps rubbing my neck, and I tilt my head to the side to give him better access.

When his lips brush against my neck, I almost explode.

I jump to my feet. "You can't tell me you want to take things slow and then do things like that!"

He laughs and shuts his laptop. "I guess I better get you home."

Mom opens the front door before I'm even halfway up the walk. "Kara—"

"I don't want to hear it," I say, pushing past her. "I'm an adult, and you of all people have no right to lecture me about what's appropriate. But, if you hadn't ripped me out of school this wouldn't even be an issue!"

My chest heaves as I rip my jacket off and toss it to the floor, followed a second later by my boots. They're covered in dirty snow that falls off the second they hit the floor, leaving little splatters of gray ice and water all over the entry.

Mom would typically freak out, but right now she doesn't even react to the shoes. She crosses her arms over her chest and shakes her head. "No way. There is no way I'm getting you another car. What happens then? I never see you again? You go off with this Derek and disappear from my life? I will not let that happen!"

For a few seconds I can't find my voice. "So you're just never going to get me another car? You're going to keep me trapped here until I forgive you? That's your brilliant plan for how to fix this?" I jerk my hand back and forth between the two of us. "Because I have to tell you, keeping me prisoner is only going to make things worse!"

"Kara." Her voice is softer, but I refuse to get sucked in.

"You can't make me feel bad about this. You've been lying to me for eighteen years—I deserve a chance to be mad for a while! Especially since you have no intention of telling me the truth."

I spin on my heel and charge up the stairs, slamming my door behind me.

It's almost two now. Derek has to be into work at three thirty, and they open at four. I have two hours to kill until I can get the hell out of here. I wish the girls hadn't left already. Right now, Derek is the only person I know who's actually in town. If only he didn't have this damn job that kept taking him away from me.

If only my dad would call.

CHAPTER TEN

I push the door of the pool hall open five minutes after four. The bell rings and Gray Beard looks up from behind the counter. When he scowls, all the pirate jokes I made the other night come back to me, and I have to bite back a smile. He really does look like a pirate, especially when he makes that face.

Derek is nowhere in sight, but I slide onto a bar stool and drop my bag to the floor by my feet anyway. Today I was smart enough to throw a few things in a duffle bag and bring them with me. I have no intention of going home.

Gray Beard doesn't come over to ask what I want, and I drum my fingers on the bar impatiently. Where is Derek?

A few minutes later, he comes out of the backroom carrying a tray loaded down with clean glasses. He doesn't look the least bit surprised to see me sitting there.

"Hey there, gorgeous. Come to take care of that tab?"

I'd forgotten all about that. "How much was it?" I unzip my purse and pull my wallet out.

Derek puts his hand on mine; the contact sends a jolt through my body. "Relax. I took care of it."

"Derek, you didn't need to do that."

"I wanted to. Besides, all those beers I paid for really worked out in my favor." He winks, and I can't help but laugh. Two minutes with him, and I'm lighter already.

Derek goes back to putting the glasses away. The second he's done he fills one up and slides it toward me. Gray Beard scowls, but doesn't say anything.

He keeps one eye on me as he wipes down the counter. "How'd it go with your mom?"

"I don't want to talk about it." I take a big drink, draining half the glass, before I put it down.

"Sorry."

"Derek," Gray Beard says, motioning for Derek to come over.

Derek gives me an apologetic smile before heading to the other side of the bar. I finish off my beer. My head is spinning already; I haven't eaten much today. Maybe I should order some food? They have appetizer type stuff here. I'm not going to make it long like this.

Derek comes back and refills my glass before I even have to ask. A couple other people come in, and he heads their way. I drink more. Between Derek and the alcohol, I'm starting to really relax. I want to drink until I forget about my mom, my dad, and the sperm donor who probably doesn't even know I exist.

When Derek returns he leans against the counter. "So what are you going to do now? Make some more phone calls?"

"I guess," I say. "If I had a car I'd just take off, you know? Go up to Kent and do some research. It would be easier up there. I wouldn't have my mom breathing down my neck, and I'd be able to think. Plus, I could go to the university library and dig up some stuff. Maybe there would be information in the yearbook or something."

Derek crosses his arms over his chest. "I'll take you."

I shake my head and the room swirls around me. "What?"

"I said, 'I'll take you.'"

"What about your job?"

"Watch this. Mike!" he calls without turning around. Gray Beard grunts and Derek yells, "I quit!"

"Fuck you!" Gray Beard yells back.

My mouth drops open and I stand up. Too fast. The room spins, and I have to grip the bar. "You can't quit your job!"

Derek puts his hand on my arm. "Sit down before you fall down."

I flop back onto the bar stool.

"I quit all the time. The job will be here when I decide I want it again. I don't really need the money. I just do this to kill time while I work on the next great American novel. You know, the next *Fifty Shades of Gray*. I'm going to call it *100 Hues of Orange*. I picked orange because it's brighter. Less predictable, you know?"

"She's British," I mumble.

His eyebrows pull together, and he stands up straight. "What?"

"The author. She's British."

"Then I guess mine will be the first great American novel!"

I'm having a hard time focusing on his words. Did he say he was willing to take me up to Kent? He's writing a novel? He *works* to kill time? Why doesn't he need money? My brain is on information overload.

I pick one question at random and throw it out there. "Are you really writing a novel?"

"No, not really. It's a graphic novel."

Graphic novel? Isn't that just a fancy word for comic book? "You mean like a comic book?"

He nods, but he doesn't look embarrassed. *Is* Derek a nerd? The *Star Wars* posters, the three video game consoles hooked up to the TV in his living room, the Syfy movie. Comic books. I pay better attention to his shirt for the first time. It says something about zombies. *The hardest part about a zombie apocalypse will be acting like I'm not excited.* He *is* a nerd! Funny I didn't notice before. Even funnier, I don't care.

Derek's telling me all about his graphic novel, and I work hard on focusing. "So these aliens have invaded and taken over most of the world, but there are still pockets of resistance fighters. My main character is this kick-ass chick who leads a group of rebels—she's totally bad-ass."

"I bet she has big boobs and wears low-cut shirts," I say, and Derek's cheeks turn red. "Derek!" I grab a few peanuts out of the bowl sitting next to me and toss them at his head. They bounce off. One hits the bar. Two land in my glass. Great.

He grins. "I am a guy!"

"And that's every guy's fantasy? A bad-ass chick with big tits who can like, what? Kick your ass or something?"

"Maybe kick life's ass. That's kind of hot." His dimple gets deeper. "Works for you anyway."

I roll my eyes. "Yeah, I'm really kicking life's ass right now. I'm a neurotic mess!"

"You're holding it together a lot better than most people would."

I look down at the bar and run my fingernail along a crack, digging it deeper. "You're the only reason I haven't gone insane yet."

"Me?"

I nod, but keep my head down. Derek puts his hand under my chin and tilts my face up. His brown eyes search mine, and just like before my body starts to relax. "You're like a drug."

He drops his hand and takes a step back. "What do you mean?"

"There's something about you, Derek. You've hit me like a Mack truck, but instead of destroying me, you somehow managed to make me *better*. I think about you all the time."

"*All* the time? Even in the shower?" I laugh and swat

at him, but he catches my wrist in his hand. "I think about you all the time too. And yes, even in the shower."

My heart races and my stomach twists, and for a second I actually hear birds chirping overhead like we're in a fairy tale and Derek has just swooped in on his white horse to save the day. It's so corny, but it's also the most amazing thing I've ever felt.

I clear my throat. "So did you really just quit your job?"

"I told you I don't need the money."

"How can you not need the money?"

Derek looks over my head. "My parents had really good life insurance. The house is paid for. No car payments. And it's not like I'm going to school or anything."

I feel like smacking myself in the forehead. "I'm sorry, that was stupid."

"You don't have to be sorry." He inhales sharply through his nose, then slowly lets it out through his mouth. "So what about Kent?"

"You were serious?"

"Yeah. I have a buddy who goes there, and he's been bugging me to come up for a visit anyway. This will give me the chance, help you to get away, and we can get some research done. Win-win!"

Win! Every second I spend with Derek, I'm more and more thankful I met him. "When do we leave?"

"When do you want to go?"

"Tomorrow morning?"

He nods and stands up straight. "Sounds good to me."

We're about an hour into our four-hour drive, and Derek is already making me squirm. He won't stop rubbing my leg, and every half hour his hand seems to move higher. Pretty soon he's going to hit *the* mark, and then I'm going to have to make him pull over so we don't have an accident.

But it is helping me relax. My insides have been churning since we got in the car. Searching for my dad seemed like a great idea in theory, but now I'm starting to get a little freaked out by what I might find. There has to be some really big, horrendous secret or my mom would tell me the truth, right?

"I came to every football game to see you cheer," Derek says, pulling me out of my thoughts.

I shift in my seat a little, so I'm facing him. "No you didn't!"

"Yup. They were the only school functions I ever attended—except prom. High school really wasn't my thing."

"I loved high school," I say wistfully. "Hanging out with my friends, flirting. It was fun and so uncomplicated." Except for Bill, but I don't say that.

Derek laughs and moves his hand to the radio, adjusting the volume. "You sure we went to the same school?"

"Beats me, I don't remember you!"

He puts his hand back on my leg—or more accurately, my thigh. This good guy bullshit is going to get old fast if he can't keep his hands off me for more than two seconds. I need to focus on something other than his fingers moving in little circles, getting closer and closer to—

"Was high school that awful for you?" I ask to distract myself.

"Not awful, just long." He glances at me out of the corner of his eye. "It was boring."

Boring? Whatever. "So no college?"

"I got into MIT, but my plans kind of changed when my family was killed."

MIT! What the hell? How smart is this guy? "You got into MIT?"

He shrugs and his hand moves to the steering wheel. He grips it tightly and stares straight ahead. "Yeah."

And here I thought I was choosing the less sensitive issue. "Is there a reason you're acting like you just confessed to a crime?"

He gives me a sideways look. "Guilt?"

"I don't understand."

"My parents were pretty thrilled when I got accepted."

"Oh." Crap. Back to the family. Now what? I hate the thought of making him sad. "You don't have to talk about any of this you know. You can tell me more about your graphic novel."

He presses his lips together for a brief second, and then his mouth slowly relaxes. But his grip on the steering wheel doesn't ease up. "That's been my distraction these past few months. I took art classes through high school, but I amped it up last summer. Since then I've been spending every free second I had drawing and writing."

"I'm so sorry, Derek." I don't know what else to say, and even that seems insignificant.

"I was supposed to be with them," he whispers.

My eyes sting, and I blink about a million times to clear the tears away. "When they had the accident?"

"They were going camping for the weekend. It was never really my thing, but I did it to humor my dad. I changed my mind at the last minute, decided to stay home and go out with—" He glances at me. "Just go out."

His girlfriend. Does he really not want me to know who she was? I could probably find out easy enough if I asked around. Maybe he thinks it will upset me. That's kind of sweet.

"You really don't have to talk about this."

He exhales and his fingers slowly ease up. After a few seconds, he moves his hand back to my leg. Even higher. Less than an inch away from the epicenter of the storm raging through me. Maybe I could just scoot a little closer...

"So what's the plan?"

I jump, and my cheeks burst into flames. Thank God

he can't read my mind! "Um…I guess go see Mark and Jeff first since we have addresses for them. If they don't know anything maybe they'll at least have an idea of someone else we can check with."

"Okay." Derek glances at the dashboard. "It's going to be almost four, by the time we get there. Dex said something about going to this sports bar for dinner then a party at his place."

I fiddle with a strand of hair. A few hours ago, I couldn't wait to find out, but now I'm anxious about the truth. Maybe a party is the best thing right now. It will help me relax and get me in the right frame of mind, so I can tackle this thing for real tomorrow.

"A party sounds good," I say. "It's not like I'm on a tight schedule or anything."

CHAPTER ELEVEN

Derek's friend turns out to be this really artsy guy who smiles *all the time*, seems to have dozens of female friends, and has a better sense of fashion than most women I know. I'd think he was gay if he wasn't so flirty—and his eyes didn't follow my ass every time I stood up. Still...

"Glad you were finally able to drag Derek up here," Dex says. He locks his front door and adjusts his glasses, thick dark frames that make his sexuality even more suspicious.

"Dex and I met when I took art classes at UD over the summer." Derek drapes his arm across my shoulder, and we head down the street. There are twelve of us in all. Dex and Derek are the only two guys, but I'm assuming there will be more at the bar. At least I hope so. These girls are all ogling Derek like he's Ryan Gosling.

This sports bar had better be close. There's too much snow to be out wandering the streets. It's piled up on both sides of the sidewalk, going up past my knees in a lot of places, and there's still about an inch covering the walkway. I'm shivering, even with Derek's arm around me. I'm not completely sure it's from the cold. Maybe I'm just nervous about learning the truth, but there's something about Kent I just don't like. It feels dark and cold. Which sounds insane, because it's winter and the reason it's dark is because it's nighttime.

Yeah, that's all it is.

A thin layer of snow dusts Dex's perfectly-in-place hair. "So you and Derek went to high school together?"

I nod, even though the story is going to make me seem totally shallow and idiotic. "I don't really remember him, though."

Dex's green eyes hold mine. He doesn't even blink. "Big schools. I went to Chaminade Julienne, so I get it. So you know Steph then?"

Derek clears his throat, and Dex's eyebrows shoot up.

"Who's Steph?" I glance at Derek, but he isn't looking at me.

"Never mind," Dex says quickly. "So you came up here to solve some mystery?"

I keep one eye on Derek. "Something like that. I need to be a lot drunker to talk about it though."

"We can take care of that!" Dex elbows me. He gets me in the ribs, and I suck in a deep breath, wincing as pain radiates across my rib cage.

"You alright?" Derek asks.

He stops walking and turns me to face him. His nose is all scrunched up and there are worry lines on his forehead. He looks so cute that I'd kiss him if I wasn't in so much pain.

I nod. "It's okay."

Dex's eyes are as big as golf balls. "What? What did I do?"

"For a smooth guy you sure are tripping all over yourself today," Derek grumbles.

With my hand still pressed to my side, I start walking again. "Forget it, let's just go." I need a drink.

The bar is packed when we walk in. The girls who came with us fan out in different directions—probably on the prowl. Dex motions for us to follow him when he heads back through the crowd, and he stops in front of an overcrowded table where four guys and two girls are sharing a few baskets of fries and mozzarella sticks. There are about a dozen glasses on the table, most empty.

Dex introduces us, and I don't miss the fact that he skips right over a girl with curly brown hair. She looks vaguely familiar, and her blue eyes snap back and forth between Derek and me. Is this Steph? I still don't know who she is, but based on the way Derek is shuffling his feet I'd guess she's his ex. Great. This trip may turn out to be a mistake.

Dex slaps Derek on the arm. "Drinks?"

Derek nods and gives me a quick—and very uncomfortable looking—smile before heading toward the bar with Dex. Leaving me alone. Normally, I'm okay with people I don't know, but the brunette's icy eyes feel like lightning bolts at the moment.

"Take a seat," a blond guy who Dex introduced as Mitch says, pulling out a chair.

I glance over my shoulder, but Derek is nowhere in sight, so I sit. The brunette is right across from me.

She holds out her hand. "Steph. Although, you probably *should* know that since we went to high school together—but I doubt you do."

Mitch laughs. He curls his fingers into claws and makes a hissing sound at Steph. "Cat fight."

I plaster a smile on my face and shake Steph's hand. "You look familiar, but it was a big school. Did we have any classes together?"

Steph's handshake is like a limp noodle. "Doubtful. I was in the AP classes."

I want to roll my eyes. "So you and Derek dated?" Clearly, Derek isn't going to tell me, but I doubt she's going to have a problem putting it all out there.

Steph nods and tosses her brown hair over her shoulder. She's cute. Kind of mousy-looking with that tiny nose and the way her mouth bunches up every time she talks to me, but she isn't a dog. Damn. It's not like I was hoping his ex would be covered in warts or anything, but would it be too much to ask that she put on a freshman fifty? Steph is tiny.

"So where are you going to college?" Mitch asks, probably to relive the tension.

"I was going to Ohio University."

"You get kicked out?" Steph snaps.

"Nooo." I stretch the word out as long as possible while all the words I want to fling at her bounce around in my head. "I was in a car accident on the way home from Christmas break. My mother decided taking a semester off would be a good idea."

Mitch laughs. "I guess you didn't agree."

"Mostly because it was her way of trapping me. Somehow when my car crashed it broke open her closet full of skeletons. She wants to keep me around until I find it in my heart to forgive her for lying to me for eighteen years."

Everyone stares at me like I just told them I tied Derek up in my red room of pain last night. I clamp my mouth shut and sit back. Okay. Too much information for strangers, I guess.

Thankfully, Derek and Dex show up with beers. Derek pulls me to my feet and plops down in the chair. When he puts his hands on my hips and guides me onto his knee, Steph's face gets redder than my red room of pain. I have to resist the urge to stick out my tongue.

"How you been, Steph?" Derek takes a sip of his beer and smiles like he doesn't notice the evil look she's giving us.

"Fine," she snaps. "I guess you got over our break up okay."

He coughs and spits beer all over me. I can't help laughing, especially when he grabs a handful of napkins and starts wiping the front of my shirt, paying special attention to my boobs.

I swat his hands away halfheartedly. "Derek, it's fine."

He tosses the napkins on the table. His brown eyes swim with mischief, and he doesn't look away from me when he says, "We broke up six months ago, Steph."

Mitch leans over, practically sticking his head between Derek and me. "Don't you know you're supposed to spend the rest of your life pining after your exes? I thought everyone knew that."

"Personally, I like to keep a bottle of Tabasco with me, just in case I run into one of my exes," Dex says. "One tiny drop in the eye and the tears start flowing like Niagara Falls."

I'm still not sure if those exes are male or female, but the comment helps thaw the atmosphere. Steph doesn't ease up though, and I have a feeling if she wasn't wedged in so tight she'd storm off.

We order dinner and more beer, and by the time we walk home I have enough alcohol in me to ward off the cold. Derek and I walk at the back of the pack. His arm is around my shoulders, and my fingers are laced through his. My face is warm and it gets even warmer when he leans down and kisses my head. I exhale. The steam rises up and gets swept away. Snow flurries are falling gently from the sky, and even though I'm tired of the snow it's pretty.

Derek pulls out a pack of cigarettes. I vaguely remember him smoking that first night we were together, but I haven't seen him do it since then. "You smoke?"

"Sometimes, when I drink. Do you care?"

I wrinkle my nose. "I've never really been a big fan of smoking, but they're your lungs I guess."

He takes his arm off my shoulder, so he can light one. "You didn't care that first night."

"In all fairness, I was pretty drunk."

"Oh, I know," he says with a wink. He takes a long drag then blows it into the air. "Seriously though, if you care, I don't have to do it."

My head is a little fuzzy. Maybe I'll mind when I'm sober. "Whatever."

When we get back to the house, Dex hands me another beer, and I take it even though I'm sure I've had enough. They crank up the music, and Derek and I snuggle on the couch. It's the most relaxed I've been in weeks.

Mitch and an Asian girl—Debbie, I think—sit down across from us.

"So I'm anxious to hear more about these skeletons," Mitch says, taking a sip of his beer.

Derek stops with his can less than an inch from his mouth. "Skeletons?"

"I was just filling everyone in on my family's dark past."

Mitch scoots closer, and a couple on the other couch stop talking so they can listen in.

"I'm even more intrigued than before," Mitch says.

"It's probably less dramatic than I'm making it sound." I squeeze the beer can and the aluminum crinkles under my fingers. "Thanks to an incompetent nurse, I recently found out that my dad isn't really my dad. Not only that, but my dad had no idea, and my mom is a big fat liar."

Dex sits down in the chair across from us. "So who's your real dad?"

I squeeze the can tighter. "Your guess is as good as mine. My mom has decided that it isn't important for me to know where I come from."

More people crowd around. If my head wasn't so foggy, I might care that I'm spilling my secrets to a room full of strangers. But Derek is next to me, and I have a very nice buzz on, so I don't give a shit.

Pretty soon guessing who my dad might be becomes the game of the night. It probably should make me cry, but instead it helps me relax. I actually find I'm enjoying all the speculation.

People throw out all the usual theories to start with—that he was married, he was a druggie, he was in witness protection and had to move. Then they get a little more creative, and suddenly he's the leader of a cult that brainwashed my mom into loving him.

"He could be famous!" Debbie exclaims suddenly. "Have any famous people ever gone to Kent?"

"I'll check!" a blonde girl yells, pulling out a cell phone.

"Maybe it's like a movie and your dad was the prince of some small country, and if he stayed with your mom he'd have to give up his throne." Dex is really into this game. So far, he's come up with the most creative theories.

"I hope it's not something that cheesy!" I say, laughing. "Although if that is what happened maybe they'll make a Lifetime movie about it."

Dex purses his lips and his eyes sweep over my face. "If they did who would play you?"

Mitch holds his hands up. "I know! Miley Cyrus for sure."

"What?" I shove him. "I don't think so!"

"You are so *Hannah Montana* material," Dex says. "I can see it!"

"I got it, I got it! Michael Keaton and Drew Carey went to Kent!" The blonde girl laughs and waves her cell phone in the air.

"Yes!" Mitch says. "Now I can see it." He plucks Dex's glasses off his face. "Put these on and you'll be the spitting image of Drew Carey."

I push him away. "He's too old! Plus, there's no way my mom would have slept with Drew Carey!"

Derek elbows my arm. "Maybe he was here for some alumni event, and they had a torrid affair. She tried to stay away from him, but she couldn't—the glasses were just too much for her. Then she found out she was pregnant, so she had to break up with him because she didn't want you raised in Hollywood."

"There's your Lifetime movie!" Mitch says, clapping. "I can see it now: *Drew Carey's Lovechild*."

"Maybe it isn't someone famous," Steph snaps. Her

lower lip is jutting out like a toddler who was just told she couldn't have candy for breakfast. "Maybe your mom doesn't want you to know because it was someone awful. Like that serial killer."

My insides tighten, and I'm suddenly torn between the desire to hurl and the urge to punch her right on her scrunched up nose. Wanting to punch her makes perfect sense. But why this sudden ache in my stomach? It can't be dread. So, it's got to either be the alcohol or a reaction to being around to Steph.

"Right. He took time away from killing students so he could go out on a date with Kara's mom—sounds likely." Mitch rolls his eyes and turns back to me. "Do you ever have the urge to kill someone?"

Steph scowls and it suddenly strikes me as funny, the way she's working so hard to make me uncomfortable. The laughter shakes my body, making my side ache, but I'm in too good a mood to let it bother me. I take another drink.

Dex snaps his fingers. "You know the governor went to Kent? What year are we talking about?"

The governor? Wouldn't that be something! "I was born in 1996, so it would have been around '95."

Dex scratches his chin. "That's the right timeframe. Maybe that's why your mom won't tell you. You're their love child, and he paid her off."

"But he wasn't governor back then," Derek notes.

Dex points his beer at Derek. "But he was planning on going into politics. It's possible." He squints and leans closer, then shakes his head. "Nope, I'm with Mitch. It's got to be Drew Carey."

I lean forward to shove Dex and a sharp pain stabs me in the ribs before traveling down my side. I wince, and Derek's smile disappears.

He practically throws his beer on the table and puts his hand on my back. "Are you alright?"

The laughter dies down. "No, no," I say, waving my

hand in the air and clutching my side. "Don't stop partying because of me. It's just a bruised spleen—nothing important."

But it doesn't stop hurting, and after a few seconds Derek helps me to my feet. "Come on."

He leads me into the kitchen, and the music and laughter fade away. The ache is slowly fading too, but little beads of sweat have broken out across my forehead.

"You're not all right," Derek says.

He shakes his head and it reminds me of my grandmother, the way she used to hover over my dad when we had dinner, watching to make sure he ate every single bite she'd put on his plate. But that wasn't really my grandmother, was it? It was just some woman my mom had tricked me into thinking was my grandmother.

My shoulders slump and I lean against the counter, suddenly drained of every ounce of energy.

"What?" Derek asks. "What's wrong?"

I wave my hand at him. "Nothing more than usual. Don't worry, I'm not hurting anymore."

"Was this a bad idea? Coming here? It's been kind of tense, with Steph and then all the questions. I thought maybe it would make it easier to joke about it. Was I wrong?" His eyebrows are pulled together, and he looks so concerned. It's cute and helps ease some of the agony clutching my heart.

"No, it was a nice distraction, and I had a good time." I slump against the kitchen counter, still rubbing my side. "It just didn't stop reality from crashing back, that's all."

"Come here," Derek says, holding his arms out.

I lean my head against his chest and he wraps his arms around me, stroking my hair like I'm a kitten. My eyes close and I start to relax, but when his hand runs down my back and stops on my hip, everything heats up. No one has ever had this effect on me. The pain and resentment are still buried inside, but this thing with Derek is bigger. Bigger than the hurt and more than a distraction. It won't erase the problems, but it helps.

"Where are we sleeping tonight?" I whisper against his chest.

"Why? You anxious to go to sleep?"

"Not to sleep."

When I look up, he's staring at me. Before I can talk myself out of it, I stand on my tiptoes and press my lips to his. It's just like that first night outside the pool hall. He groans and pushes me against the fridge. He cups my face in his hands, and his tongue attacks my mouth. Then his hand moves down. Down my neck and shoulder, over my breast to my stomach. His fingers nudge my shirt up and tickle the bare skin above my jeans, staying there for just a second before slipping underneath. When his hand cups my breast, it's like adding wood to a fire.

"Derek," I whisper against his lips.

My hand moves down his chest until I reach the button on his jeans. I undo the button, and when his teeth nip at my bottom lip, it only makes things more intense. His thumb moves over my nipple and I gasp when the flames grow stronger. Slowly I unzip his jeans, and he pulls away, looking down at me as my fingers play with the waistband of his boxer briefs.

"Shit," someone says from the doorway.

We both spin around to face Steph. Her face is brighter than a stop light, and her icy eyes flicker between the two of us then down as she takes in Derek's unzipped fly. It isn't until her eyes get bigger than golf balls that I realize Derek still has his hand up my shirt—on my boob!

When she purses her lips, she looks more like a mouse than ever before. "Right in the middle of the kitchen? Nice."

She stomps out of the room. Derek and I just stand there for a few seconds with our mouths hanging open. Then I burst out laughing. I can't help it. The way her nose was all scrunched up and her eyes were huge, she reminded me of a scared little animal.

Derek grins. "Glad you can laugh about that."

"Can't you?"

He shrugs. He still hasn't moved his hand.

"Um, Derek, did you know your hand was still on my boob?"

"I know. You weren't complaining so I thought I'd just keep it there from now on." He blinks, trying to look all innocent. "No?"

"Probably not the best place to keep it. It's not really the same as a pocket."

He gives my boob a quick squeeze and drops his hand. "I had to try," he says, zipping his pants.

"I guess we go back out to the living room now?"

He points to his crotch. "Probably should give it a few minutes."

I press my lips together, but it doesn't work, the laugh pops out of my mouth anyway. "That might be a good idea."

CHAPTER TWELVE

The sun may still be low in the sky, but it is way too bright after last night's party. And Derek is driving too slowly. Why isn't he going faster? When we left Dex's I told him I needed caffeine ASAP. I thought he understood the severity of the situation.

"I can't believe Dex doesn't have coffee," I grumble, sinking lower in the passenger seat.

Derek yawns and shakes his head like he's trying to keep himself awake. "He's a tea drinker."

Gay for sure. "Whatever. Just get me to Starbucks before I kill someone."

We're only two blocks from Dex's apartment when Derek abruptly pulls over and puts the car in park. He must think I'm joking, because I don't see a Starbucks sign anywhere.

"I need caffeine, Derek."

He elbows my arm. I glare at him and rub it, but he just rolls his eyes and points to the building in front of us. "Look."

Kent Coffee. Holy crap.

When I don't move he leans over and opens my door

for me. "You were much happier the last two mornings."

"We were both almost naked on those mornings. Makes a difference."

He chuckles and jumps out. "I don't see how. It's not like anything happened."

Does he seriously not know how sexy I think he is?

When we step into the coffee shop, I inhale the heavenly aroma of caffeine. If they could inject it straight into my veins I'd let them. Until then, a large white chocolate mocha will have to do.

Three steps in and I freeze. Steph stands on the other side of the room with an apron on. "Did you know she worked here?"

Derek's eyebrows pull together, and he looks around. When his eyes land on Steph, he swears under his breath. I guess not. He grabs my hand and starts to pull me toward the door. "We can go somewhere else."

I pull my hand out of his. "No way! I want coffee and I don't care if Ted Bundy comes back from the dead to serve it to me. I'm getting it."

I go to the nearest empty table and throw myself into a chair. There are two waitresses. Steph and a blonde who looks like she's had one too many shots of espresso. Hopefully, we get blondie.

Derek sinks into the chair across from me. He's pouting.

"What's the big deal? So she walked in on us kissing. Who cares?"

He sinks lower, like that will make him invisible or something. "I don't like her being so pissed at me. I didn't do anything to her. She broke up with me."

I sit up straighter, trying to catch blondie's eye. How long does it take to get a damn waitress to come to your table? I'm starting to get the shakes. "It's a girl thing. We're complicated."

Derek snorts. "That's an understatement."

Blondie finishes taking an order and glances our way.

She smiles, and my shoulders start to relax when she heads toward us. But she stops next to Steph and tilts her head in our direction. Crap. Steph's face hardens when her eyes meet mine. Maybe she'll tell blondie to take the table? Nope. Blondie heads to the kitchen, and Steph walks toward us.

"Morning. You two decide to make today just as crappy as yesterday?"

Derek gets up. "I'll wait outside."

"Coward," I hiss, but he keeps walking. Whatever, I'm getting my coffee. "Large white chocolate mocha for me and…" I bite my lip. He's had his coffee black the past two mornings while I added milk and sugar.

"He takes his black," Steph snaps.

"Geez. Will you chill? I know he takes his coffee black. I just wasn't sure if he'd order something fancy in a place like this!"

She rolls her eyes. "Derek isn't really the *fancy* type."

I get the feeling that there's supposed to be an insult in that statement, but I have no idea what. "Okay. A large coffee for him then. Both to go."

Steph sighs or snorts or grunts, I'm not really sure which one, and turns away. She seems fun.

I flip on my phone as soon as she's gone. There's another text from my mom. She's already sent two this morning wanting to know where I am. I didn't exactly tell her I was going out of town—just that I was going to be with Derek. Should I tell her I'm in Kent? What will she do? The odds that she'd drive up here to stop me are pretty slim, but I still don't want to give her a chance. I think I'll keep my exact location a mystery until I have a little more information.

Kara: *Went out of town with Derek. Visiting some of his friends. B home in a day or 2. Don't worry.*

She's going to love that.

Steph is back in record time. I pull out a ten-dollar bill, but before I can get up she sits in the other chair. "Don't hurt him."

What is her problem? "Who says I'm going to hurt him?"

She rolls her eyes and I cross my fingers, hoping they get stuck that way. No such luck. "Oh come on! You can't seriously tell me you like him? You were a cheerleader in high school."

This feels just like one of those cheesy teen movies. I pause to see if someone is going to yell cut. "In case you haven't noticed, Steph, high school is over. What's your deal, anyway? You broke up with Derek. Why are you being such a bitch just because he's seeing someone else?"

"I didn't *want* to break up with Derek. I was in love with him." She sighs. "You know about his family, right?"

In love with him? Great, now I'm in for it. "Yes. We've talked about it."

"Well we were together when it happened. I was with him when he made the funeral arrangements, and I held his hand at the graveside. I was there for him." She stares at the floor, and I just pray she keeps her eyes down. If she cries, I'm going to start feeling bad for her, and I *don't* want that to happen.

"I'm not following you. What does any of that have to do with me?"

"It doesn't. It has to do with Derek. He was never the same after that."

Now I roll my eyes. Hello, Captain Obvious! "He lost his family. Can you blame him for being a little depressed?"

She finally looks up and just like I thought, there are tears in her eyes. Damn. "It was more than depression." She grabs her ponytail, which reminds me of a Brillo pad pulled back like that, and twists it around her hand. "It was like he wanted to be a different person. He changed his mind about MIT, stopped speaking to his friends, got contacts and new clothes. He even quit all the programming stuff he'd always loved and started focusing on that magazine—"

"Graphic novel," I correct.

"Whatever. I hate that thing! He would have stopped talking to me too if I'd let him. But I went over every night to see him, hoping that he'd snap out of it. But he'd just sit there in his Dad's office, drawing. Ignoring me."

She sniffs and there it is! Sympathy. Crap. "I'm sorry, Steph, that really sucks."

"Yeah, it does. I managed to convince him to go to prom with me." She looks down at her hands. "And I even slept with him, hoping that would bring him back. But it didn't."

Is she telling me that to make me uncomfortable? If she is, the joke's on her. I already knew they had sex. Not that hearing it doesn't make my stomach clench.

A tear slides down her cheek, and she wipes it away. "Anyway, I didn't mean to tell you all that." Sure she didn't. "I just wanted you to know that he isn't as strong as he acts."

Steph gets to her feet, and I put the money on the table and grab the cups. She doesn't move, almost like she wants to make sure I actually leave. I take two steps to the door and stop. Maybe it will make her feel better? Do I *want* her to feel better?

I turn, but not completely, and I don't look her in the eye. "I really do like him, you know. It's been a while since I dated...not since Bill Harper." I swallow. "There's something about Derek..." I shrug. "Just thought you should know."

She doesn't say anything, so I head toward the door. Should I tell Derek about my conversation with Steph? Probably not. At least not now. Maybe another time.

"Steph give you a hard time?" Derek takes the lid off his coffee and blows into the steaming cup.

"Nope. Just a few dirty looks."

He gives me a skeptical look, but before he can accuse me of being a liar my phone beeps. I pull it out and cringe. Mom.

Mom: *You went away with this boy? That is not acceptable Kara.*

Apparently she still thinks I'm eleven.

Kara: *I'm an adult.*

She's sure to text me back in a minute, but I don't want to read it. I turn my phone off and focus on my coffee. The first sip goes straight to my brain.

"Okay, so we're off to…" Derek glances down at his phone, propped up on the cup holders. "AlphaMicron to see this Mark guy. Not sure what that is."

I grab his phone and pull up the Web site. "Says they perform research and development for the Department of Defense."

"Great, so basically it's going to be just like Cyberdyne Systems in the *Terminator* movies."

"Never saw them."

He shakes his head in disapproval.

I roll my eyes. Dating a nerd is more complicated than I thought it would be. "Um…I'm pretty sure the first two were made before I was born!"

"Doesn't matter. They're classic sci-fi. I'm going to have to force you to watch them all. Even the third one, which kind of sucked."

I cringe into my coffee cup. "Is it going to be like that gator movie from the other day?"

Derek laughs. "No! Those are just stupid Syfy movies. They're good for a laugh."

"Good because I don't think I could sit through three of those movies."

"Four. There are four *Terminator* movies."

Sweet. I go back to my coffee.

"So you're not into sci-fi," Derek says, drumming his fingers on the steering wheel. "You probably like those sappy chick movies that make you cry, right?"

I wrinkle my nose. "No. I like funny movies. Something that I don't have to think about too hard. Something that's purely for entertainment."

He nods his head slowly. "I can do that."

I can't help smiling when I take another sip of my coffee. "And I guess I can watch your robot movies."

Derek gives me one of his adorable grins as he pulls into the parking lot. He could get me to do about anything just by flashing me that smile.

AlphaMicron is huge building made of tan bricks with lots of shiny glass windows. It does look like something from the future.

"This place seems pretty important." Derek studies the building as we make our way across the parking lot. "We might not be able to just waltz in and see this guy."

"Maybe we can make an appointment? It's worth a shot anyway."

The reception area is brightly lit thanks to the dozens of windows, and the furniture is all white and stiff. Very uncomfortable looking. Just like the outside of the building, it gives off a futuristic vibe. This seems like a place where scientists would feel at home.

A woman in a crisp black suit sits behind the desk. She barely glances at us when we walk up, even though there's no one else in the room, and it's eerily quiet. Usually places like this play music for visitors, but this building is as silent as a cemetery. It makes me squirm; they don't exactly give off a welcoming vibe.

We stop in front of the desk and I clear my throat, and the woman finally glances up. "Can I help you?" Her blonde hair is slicked into a tight bun. Her gray eyes snap back and forth between me and Derek before moving down over our clothes and then up to our faces. Finally settling on me. She frowns.

"We were hoping to see Mark Hilton." I stand as straight as possible, but her frown only deepens.

"Dr. Hilton is a very busy man." She glances down at her computer and types a few things in. "No appointment I'm guessing."

"No." I glance at Derek, but he just grins.

She shakes her head and types and clicks her tongue like we're the most annoying thing she's ever had to deal with. Based on how empty this place seems, maybe we are.

"Dr. Hilton can see you tomorrow at nine in the morning." Her eyes flick up. "Sharp."

"Sounds good." I'd like to see him today, but tomorrow is better than nothing.

She clicks her tongue again. "What's your name?"

"Kara Jones and Derek Miller."

Her mouth turns down even more when she types it in. "Nine on the dot."

I paste a smile on my face and stick my hand in my pocket, so I don't give her the finger. "We'll be here!"

"She was friendly," Derek says when we're safely outside.

"Yeah. It must be loads of fun working there."

He puts his arm around me and kisses the side of my head. "Where to now?"

"Grace's ex?" I pull my notebook out of my purse and flip it open. "Jeff Hayes—works at Fifth Third bank."

The bank is crowded and we have to wait in line behind six other people. Derek hums the whole time, and I can't help thinking about what Steph said. He seems fine. He talks about his family. He lives in the house—it's not like he isn't dealing with it. But maybe there is something to what she said. He is different than he was in high school. So much that no one ever recognizes him. So maybe he wants to be someone else, is that so wrong? Who wouldn't want to pretend to be someone else after going through something like that?

Derek elbows me and tilts his head toward a man with brown hair and a porn star mustache who just came out of the vault. He crosses the room and takes a seat at a desk. The nameplate in front of him says, *Jeff Hayes, Loan Officer.*

"Guess we don't need to be in this line," I say.

Derek and I duck under the rope divider. He's so tall that he almost knocks the whole thing down, and I catch it just before it falls. Giggling like crazy.

"Ha, ha," he says. But he's laughing too. Maybe I'm as much therapy for him as he is for me?

Jeff Hayes is staring at us when I turn around. I smooth down my jacket and stand up straight, trying my best to look like a responsible member of society. For some reason, he frowns.

"Jeff Hayes?" I say hesitantly, even though his name is right in front of me.

"Can I help you?" His mustache bobs up and down when he talks, and it reminds me of a fuzzy caterpillar sleeping on his upper lip.

"My name is Kara Jones. My parents are Charlotte and Greg Jones—I think you know them from your time at Kent."

"Grace told me about your call yesterday when I dropped our son off. Please, have a seat." His mustache jumps when he talks. His fuzzy upper lip is distracting, but he seems nice enough. He isn't telling me to get lost, so that's a good sign.

Jeff doesn't crack a smile when Derek and I sit. Great. Maybe it isn't good news. "I have to say, Grace was pretty pissy yesterday. She accused me of being your father."

My mouth drops open and I shake my head, half-standing. "Oh my gosh, Mr. Hayes I'm so sorry! I never implied that!"

He waves his hand in the air, and I sit back down. "Forget it. She's always pissy when I stop by." He runs his thumb and forefinger across his mustache like a villain. A villain in a porno. "I was surprised to hear about your mom, though. Grace never really liked her that much—probably jealousy—but to me, she was always sweet. Your parents did go through a rough patch, but it never would have occurred to me that she was cheating on Greg. In fact, when they got back together and I heard she was pregnant, I assumed the whole thing was just hormones. Or fear. An unplanned pregnancy can do that." He frowns like he knows from experience.

My whole body slumps. "So you have no idea who my father is?" I don't mean to sound so dejected, but I can't help it.

Jeff gives me a sympathetic look. "I'm sorry. I do know that your mom's old roommate Kelly Duncan still lives in the area." He clears his throat and scribbles something on a piece of paper before handing it to me. "She and I have gone out a few times, but Grace doesn't know. So if you see my ex-wife again, you didn't hear that from me."

Good Lord. I guess I'm not the only one who has to worry about family drama. Although, I did escape it for eighteen years.

I take the paper and glance at it. Kelly's work address. "Thanks, Mr. Hayes."

"Wish I could tell you more, I really do. I can't imagine what you and your dad are going through right now. Greg and I used to be real close—I actually stood up with him at the Justice of the Peace when your parents got married. Never could figure out why he and your mom stopped talking to us. I blamed Grace actually. She can be a real bitch sometimes."

I pull Derek to his feet and smile at Jeff—I want to get out of here before he starts telling us about his divorce. "Thanks again!"

"So now we go see this Kelly woman," Derek says once we're back in the car.

Maybe I shouldn't be dragging him all over the place like this. He can't be having a good time, not unless he enjoys being around other people's drama. "I'm sorry. Is this boring for you?"

He grins and starts the car. "No. I'm having fun because I'm with you. I wish it were under better circumstances, but…" He takes my hand and his thumb traces small circles on my palm. "I like being with you."

"I like being with you too."

His brown eyes search mine and my heart thumps like a car racing down the Audubon. I wouldn't be surprised if it broke out of my chest and took off down the road.

"I'm going to kiss you now," he says. "Sorry if I have coffee breath."

His hand goes to the back of my neck, and he pulls me closer. The gesture is possessive or needy or hungry—and so hot. I scoot closer to him and end up hitting my knee.

"Ouch." I pull away. "This damn car is too small!"

Derrick puts the car in drive. "Keeps me honorable."

If he keeps teasing me like this, I'm going to tell him to shove his honor up his ass.

"Let's go see Kelly." I squirm in my seat. All he has to do is look at me, and I'm hot all over.

He laughs and backs out of the parking space. "Those are quite the mood swings."

"I'm sexually frustrated."

"Isn't the guy supposed to be the one begging for it?"

"You'd think."

CHAPTER THIRTEEN

The address turns out to be a small bookstore. When we walk in, the only person there is a woman with light brown hair cut shorter than Derek's. She watches us approach, drumming her fingers on the counter.

"You must be Charlotte's daughter, I can see the resemblance." When I give her a questioning look, she shrugs. "Jeff called me."

At least I don't have to explain why I'm here. "He said you and my mom were roommates?"

"Look, your mom and I lived together out of convenience. We weren't really friends. But—" She pauses dramatically and both Derek and I step forward. "I did know she had someone on the side. I wish I could tell you who it was, but I can't. She never mentioned it to me. I just overheard her talking on the phone once."

Her eyes narrow on my face. "Look, this might not be any of my business, but are you sure you want to find out who your father is? I know Jeff told you that your mom went through a *rough patch*, but it was more than that. She was like a different person. Maybe she has a very good reason for keeping you in the dark."

"No, I have to know."

She sighs and slides a piece of paper across the counter. "Here are a few names you could check out. They're people I remember her mentioning or that stopped by the apartment to study." She points to a name on the list and I lean closer: Dan Davis. "This guy she even dated right before your dad. Maybe they hooked up once after that? I pulled up the alumni page and wrote down the addresses for a few of them. That's the best I can do."

When she finishes talking, she crosses her arms over her chest. I guess she's in a hurry to get us out of here. At least she was willing to help.

I stare at the paper and for a second I can't speak. My heart is pounding, but I'm not sure if it's excitement or fear. There are nine names on it! One of these men could be my dad. "This is amazing, thank you."

She rolls her eyes. "No problem. Family is a bitch."

Oh my gosh! More drama? Maybe my situation isn't as insane as I think it is.

Derek and I huddle together at a small table in the corner of Starbucks, going over the list. We're able to eliminate a few people pretty fast. Like Rishi Desai, who's Indian, and Tim Hall and Jason Michaels, who are both black. Despite my dark hair, there's nothing ethnic-looking about me. Kelly didn't have last names for two of the men, Doug and someone that went by JJ, and one more wasn't listed on the alumni page. Unfortunately, his name is also Jason Simpson. A less common name would have been nice. It might as well be John Smith!

"I think we start with this Dan Davis guy. He lives in Texas and there's a phone number. You should just call him," Derek says. "He's your mom's ex, so it's a good place to start."

Calling isn't ideal, makes it too easy for the person to

hang up on me, but since I'm not going to Texas anytime soon…

"Makes sense," I say, pulling out my phone.

I have three text messages. My mom, Megan and Dee. I'll deal with them later. Now I need to make this phone call before I chicken out. Having the names in front of me makes me feel like we're getting closer, and for some reason it makes me want to hurl. Calling Grace to ask questions was one thing—she can't be my dad—but one of these guys might actually be my biological father.

I dial the number and hit send, then hold my breath when it starts to ring. Once, twice—voicemail picks up. He must have hit ignore.

It beeps and I take a deep breath. "Hi, my name is Kara Jones. Um…" Crap. What do I say? Derek waves his hand in the air, so I just blurt it out. "You dated my mom, Charlotte Myer, back at Kent State. Anyway, I was just calling because I had a random question about the past. If you could call me back when you get a free minute I'd really appreciate it. Thanks!"

I hit end and practically drop the phone on the table. "Well that was awkward. I hope he calls back."

"If he doesn't it could mean he's actually your dad."

My stomach drops. Why do I have this feeling of dread hanging over me? It can't be that bad, can it? "True. Of course if that's the case, it sucks. He lives all the way in Texas. It's not like we can just drop by his house or anything!"

"We'll just have to hope he calls back then." Derek picks the paper up. "There's this Ian guy who lives in California. You want to call him next?"

Might as well get this over with. "I'm going to need a drink after this," I mumble while dialing the number.

"I think we can take care of that."

Someone answers on the first ring, but after a few awkward seconds of me explaining who I am, he tells me he doesn't remember my mom. I'd think he was lying—

and maybe he is my father—except he asks me a few questions like he isn't sure. Five minutes later, after accepting he really doesn't know who my mom is, I thank him and hang up. Well, that's one more off the list.

I scratch the name out. "Who's next?"

Derek tilts his head toward my phone. "Aren't you going to text your mom back?" I shrug, and one corner of his mouth turns down. "Okay. It's time for me to play the orphan card."

My stomach twists and I have no idea what to say. This is coming from out of nowhere.

"I totally get why you're pissed, Kara. Anybody would be. But she's still your mom, and she's alive. You need to try to forgive her. Whatever her reasons were, even if you don't agree with them, she has been a good mom. Right?"

"Yeah."

"And you had a good childhood. She loved you?"

Damn. I hate that he's right. "Okay. I get it."

I pick up the phone and stare at it for a moment before opening her text.

Mom: *Please answer me. I just want to make sure you're OK.*

Well now I feel like scum. Do I call her or text her? If I call just hearing her voice might make me angry again. Better stick with the texts for now.

Kara: *I'm OK. Sorry 4 not texting. Will keep you updated. Might B a few more days.*

I almost type love you at the end—old habit—but I can't bring myself to do it, so I just hit send. Baby steps.

Derek pats my hand. "Sorry I had to be an ass."

"No. You were right. This whole thing sucks, but she's still my mom." And my dad is still my dad. I just wish he knew it.

On impulse, I start another text, this time to my dad.

Kara: *Still want 2 C U. Out of town right now, maybe when I get back in a few days we can get together?*

I don't have a lot of hope he'll answer, but I hit send anyway before checking the texts from the girls. Megan is just texting to make sure I'm alright, and Dee to make suggestive comments about Derek. I guess she's really hoping things won't work out between us. I bite back a smile and send her a quick reply.

Kara: *Keep your hands off or I'll cut U!*

Derek grins when I look up. "Okay, so we still have this guy in New York."

"Let's get it over with."

I dial and wait, and just when I think the voicemail is going to pick up a man answers. "Um, is this Vinnie Castellano?"

"Yup. Who's this?" He has a Brooklyn accent, and all I can picture is one of the Sopranos.

I take a deep breath and blurt it out just like before. "Hi, my name is Kara Jones. I think you know my mom from when you attended Kent University. Charlotte Meyer?"

"Yeah, I remember your mom. Been a long time."

"So this may be a little awkward, but I was wondering if it's possible the two of you ever had a fling?"

Vinnie laughs and I relax. If he is my dad, he doesn't have any bad memories of her. "Not awkward, just a little funny. I actually had a thing for your mom. Asked her out a few times, but she was dating this guy…" I hold my breath. Could this be it? "Greg something." Crap. "Then they broke up and I thought I'd give it another shot. 'Course then she was hung up on some other guy. I think she got back together with that Greg fella though."

"She did," I say, practically jumping up and down. "But this other guy, do you have any idea who the other guy was?"

"Never met him, but he called her a few times when we were studying. Name was JJ or something like that."

I grab the paper and put a big circle around JJ. That has to be him! "You don't remember anything else about him?"

"Nope, sorry. What's this all about anyway?"

"Um, just trying to surprise her with something."

"You mean like a long lost love or something like that?"

Sounds good to me! "Yeah, exactly like that."

"Just like a movie," he mutters. "Well, I wish I could say it was me, but I'd put my money on this JJ guy."

I thank him a million times before ending the call.

"So JJ?" Derek asks.

"Yup. Only he has no idea who the guy is."

"This guy." Derek points to the list and his finger lands on Jason Simpson. "His first name starts with a J. Maybe it was a nickname?"

"I could kiss you!"

"Don't let the fact that we're in public stop you."

The smile that spreads across my face has to make me look like the Cheshire Cat from *Alice in Wonderland*.

I lean forward and wiggle my finger at him. "Come here."

Derek and I have the apartment to ourselves since Dex has a date—I don't know *who* it's with—and we're laying on the futon in the living room watching reruns of *Firefly* on the Syfy channel. He was outraged when I confessed I'd never seen it. I'm starting to accept the fact that I'm going to have to learn to really like sci-fi if I want to be with Derek. And I do. Want to be with Derek, that is. The sci-fi thing is still a little iffy.

My head is on his chest, and he's playing with my hair, and all I want to do is kiss him. But he keeps making a big deal about taking things slow. Maybe it has something to do with Steph.

"Steph did talk to me a little," I say out of nowhere.

Derek stiffens. "What did she say?"

"She told me not to hurt you." I expect him to laugh—even now it sounds so ridiculous. But he doesn't relax.

"Is that all?"

I prop my head up with my arm, so I can see his face, but he doesn't look at me. He's studying the ceiling like we're in the Sistine Chapel instead of a dirty college apartment.

"Derek, are you alright?"

"She must have said something else." He still won't look at me, and his voice is flat. Just like it was when he told me his parents and brother were dead.

"She just said that you're different now."

He practically pushes me away and rolls off the futon. "That crap again."

"I'm sorry, Derek. I wouldn't have brought it up if I thought it was going to bother you."

He paces the room like a caged animal looking for a way to escape. I don't know what happened.

"She went on and on about that after my family died. Like I *could* have been the same person after that!" He runs his hand through his hair and throws himself into a rickety chair that wobbles under his weight.

I sit up, but don't go over to him. He stares at the floor, and he looks so sad. I have no idea what to do about it.

"I'm sorry," I whisper.

My throat burns and I know any moment the tears are going to explode out of me. I've been holding them back for too long. Every text I get from my mom, every text I don't get from my dad, it's all fodder for the tsunami of emotions building up inside me. Before long it's going to strike and wipe me out completely.

Derek's head jerks up, and his eyes soften. He crosses to the futon and sits down next to me. "No, I'm sorry. That wasn't about you." He studies the back of his hand. "She tried to be supportive; I know she did. But it was too much. She was always there, and she questioned everything I did. She didn't like any of the choices I was making and all I was doing was trying to deal with it all the best that I could."

He throws himself back and stares at the ceiling so intently that I almost turn to look. "She didn't understand why I was changing myself. She thought I wasn't dealing with things—that I was in denial. That wasn't it. I didn't want to forget who I was or try to block out my family, I needed other people to forget who I was. That was the worst part. None of it was private. Everyone knew what had happened and every time I left the house I had to deal with more well-meaning people. They always asked how I was holding up, if I needed anything. But all I wanted was for them to leave me alone so I could deal with it. It got easier once people stopped recognizing me."

Derek closes his eyes and turns his head to the side. I run my fingers down his cheek, caressing his face. His eyes open, and he grabs my hand and presses it to his lips. A shiver runs up my arm and through my body.

We lay like that for a while. His head rests on my chest as Captain Reynolds and his crew fly from planet to planet, fighting bad guys and dodging trouble. The show's okay. I guess I could get into sci-fi if it's like this.

We're halfway through our second episode when Derek starts running his hand up and down my thigh. I try to focus on the TV, but it's impossible with his fingers moving like that. Tension builds in my body until I start to squirm. When I glance down, Derek stares at me. His eyes hold mine for a few seconds. Without a word, he sits up. He grabs my face between his hands, and pulls me toward him, and his mouth is on mine, hot and needy. Desperate. He parts my lips with his tongue as I run my hands down his spine to the hem of his shirt, and he breaks away long enough for me to yank it over his head. As soon as it's gone his mouth is on mine. He pushes me onto my back and his lips move down my neck to my collar bone, his tongue tracing the little dip at the base of my throat while his hands move up my stomach, under my shirt. Just like last night, I moan when his hand reaches my breast. Only this time there's no one to interrupt us. I rake my fingernails down his spine when he pulls my bra aside, gasping when his fingers tease my nipple.

He kisses me again, nibbling on my bottom lip.

"What happened to being a gentleman?"

He kisses his way across my cheek to my earlobe, grasps it between his teeth, and pulls on it. "This is more fun."

I can't argue with that. Not when he pulls my shirt over my head or undoes my bra. Not when his lips move lower on my body, exploring every inch of me from my neck to my stomach. Not when he unbuttons my jeans and his fingers dip inside my lacy thong.

"Derek," I gasp, squeezing my eyes shut.

The fire in my stomach transforms into a full-fledged inferno. My nails dig into his skin, and I arch my back as stars invade the darkness, bursting behind my closed eyes like it's the fourth of July. I'm panting and he never stops kissing me, never stops moving his fingers.

"Kara," he whispers against my mouth. "God, you are so beautiful."

Then the earthquake hits and I gasp, curling my toes and pulling myself closer to him, grasping his hand. My eyes fly open and his brown eyes stare back at me, bathing me in warmth and desire and more passion than I've ever felt before.

His kisses soften, and my body relaxes. When he pulls my head against his chest, I sigh without even thinking. It feels like I'm lying on a cloud.

"I would ask how that was but…" His voice dances.

My face heats up, and I pull his face to mine to kiss him.

Derek's eyes close and he takes a slow, deep breath. "Do you have any idea how good you are for me?" His warm breath brushes my skin, sending tingles down my spine. "You help me forget how shitty things have been. Not just the thing with Steph, but all of it."

My heart swells to fifty times its normal size, and I move closer. Like if I can just get close enough all the pain from the last few weeks will disappear forever. "We don't have to stop." I don't want to stop.

Derek pulls back and runs his hand through his hair. "Well, I didn't exactly come prepared."

"Oh." Crap. That blows…but that doesn't mean there aren't other things I can do. Derek needs a turn too. I bite my lip and sit up, grinning. "What about you? I wouldn't want you to think I'm selfish."

He has a giant grin on his face as he lies back, putting his hands behind his head. Geez. I giggle and hold his gaze while I undo his pants.

CHAPTER FOURTEEN

"Nine o'clock *sharp*," Derek says, snapping his fingers. He props open the front door to Dex's apartment while I slip on my shoes.

A gust of cool air blows through the living room and I shiver. I pull my jacket tighter as I get to my feet. My shoes feel like they're made of lead.

"Yeah, yeah. I'm coming." I follow him out to the car. "I wish we'd gotten up earlier so we could stop for coffee." Not that I want to bump into Steph two mornings in a row.

Derek pulls the door open for me. He's always such a gentleman. "You and your coffee." He leans toward me just as I duck into the car. "I thought you'd be in a better mood after last night."

Despite my total dislike of mornings, I can't stop a smile from curling up my lips. Last night *was* amazing. Derek must see my grin, because he winks before he shuts the door.

We waltz through the front door of AlphaMicron with exactly seven minutes to spare. The same woman is sitting at the desk wearing an almost identical black suit. Once again, she doesn't look up when we walk in. Is she supposed to scare people off? Because if that's what they hired her to do, mission accomplished.

"We have a nine o'clock appointment with Dr. Hilton," I say when we stop in front of the desk.

She glances up briefly. "Name?"

Does she really not remember us or is she just being a bitch? "Kara Jones and Derek Miller."

She nods and types more—a lot more than our names. Her lips purse and her eyebrows pull down. She looks like she just tasted something bitter. Maybe she took a big old bite out of her personality. She sure leaves a bitter taste in my mouth.

"Have a seat," she says without looking up. "I'll let him know you're here."

Derek and I make our way over to the uncomfortable looking furniture. As promised, it's stiff and awkward. No matter how I shift, my ass still hurts after thirty seconds.

Derek is squirming just as much as I am, and he keeps looking at his phone. Does he have some place to be? Waiting for a phone call? "So, if this guy can't give us any information our next step will be?"

I pull out my notebook—it's getting pretty ragged-looking—and flip it open. "We haven't checked out these Liz Winston suspects yet. We could contact a few at least."

Derek leans forward so he can get a better look. "We still don't know anything about this Brad Roth guy, either."

"And both Tobi and Paul live up in Cleveland."

Derek drums his fingers on his knee. "We could go up there. It's only an hour away."

"It's worth a shot. But hopefully Dr. Hilton will be able to tell us something, and we won't have to worry about it. My money's still on this Jason Simpson though."

Derek nods, and his hair flops over his eyebrow. He flicks his head to the side. "Maybe if we looked him up in a yearbook? We could head over to the library. See what he looked like at least."

"That's a good idea." I glance at the clock on the wall.

So much for nine *sharp*.

The minutes tick by, and I tap my toe to the beat of the second hand. It echoes through the sterile room, but the receptionist never looks up. What's her deal anyway? There's no way she forgot we're here.

By nine thirty, I've had enough. I jump up and charge over to the desk. "Our appointment was at nine. Is Dr. Hilton running late?"

She types a few things into the computer. What is that computer telling her? The answers to the universe? "Looks like you just missed him." She doesn't even look up from the screen.

"I'm sorry? Did you say we just missed him? We had an appointment!"

She finally looks up, and her icy eyes cut right through me. "Would you like to reschedule? I could get you in…tomorrow around three."

I clench my fist and I swear it starts to move on its own. It's two inches off the desk when Derek grabs my hand.

"Three sounds great."

She nods and starts typing—again! I wish I had a bat so I could pummel that computer. "Your names?"

My eyes almost bug out of my head, but before I can say anything Derek steps in. Again.

By the time we're outside my face is on fire and for once I'm thankful for the cold weather.

Derek, however, laughs his ass off. "Come on! That was funny."

I glare at him. "Funny? That woman is infuriating."

Derek puts his arm around me and pulls me toward the car. "Come on. Let's get you some coffee."

My cheeks are hot and I'm still grumbling all kinds of creative names under my breath, but I allow him to lead me to the car. I'll be in a better mood once I get my coffee. Maybe then I won't want to go back and punch that woman in the face.

We're standing in line at Starbucks when my phone rings. It's a number I don't recognize. "I'm going to step outside," I whisper to Derek before I run for the door.

The second my feet hit the icy pavement, I answer the phone.

"Is this Kara Jones?" The man's voice booms through the speaker. It makes the phone vibrate against my ear.

My heart pounds. This could be my father! "Yes it is."

"This is Dan Davis. You left me a message about your mom."

There have been too many names the past few days, and it takes me a few seconds to remember. Mom's ex—lives in Texas. "Yes! Thank you so much for calling me back. I'm so sorry to bug you, I just…" There's really no way to make this part any less awkward. "I've been contacting people from my mom's past—working on a little surprise for her. It's a long story." He has no idea. "Anyway, someone mentioned your name. I guess you dated my mom at some point?"

He clears his throat. "Uh, yeah. I dated her back in ninety-three. We went out for a few months, but it was nothing serious."

Crap. "Really? Someone told me she dated you then this other guy, but that the two of you got back together. Maybe had a little fling?" My face is hot, so I lean my forehead against the glass window. It's covered in ice, but hopefully it will help me cool down. Thank God this guy can't see me.

"Nope. That wasn't me. I actually don't know if I ever saw her again after we broke up. I started dating my wife just a few weeks later, and we've been together since. Married almost seventeen years now."

I exhale and close my eyes. So this guy isn't my dad. "Weird. Can I ask if you know someone named JJ? Or maybe Jason Simpson?"

"JJ…doesn't sound familiar. Jason Simpson though, I do remember. He and your mom were in the same graduate program."

I stand up. Maybe this is the clue we've been looking for! "Really? Do you know anything about him?"

"Nope. Just met him once or twice in passing. Sorry I can't be of any more help." Someone starts talking to him in the background, and he clears his throat. "Listen, I have a meeting I have to get to, so unless you have anything else…"

"No, I don't. Thanks for calling me back."

I head back inside, and Derek hands me a venti white chocolate mocha. "Anything?"

"He never dated my mom again, has no idea who JJ is, and even though he remembers Jason he couldn't give me a single detail."

Derek gives my hand a reassuring squeeze. "Library?"

I take a big sip—Okay, maybe it's more of a gulp. "Might as well."

Thankfully, there's an index in the back of the yearbook. The first thing we do is look up Jason Simpson. Too bad it doesn't really help. There are a few pictures of him at school functions, but that's it.

"His hair is dark like mine, but that doesn't mean anything. So is my mom's." I lean closer and squint like it will somehow make the blurry black and white face clearer. "You think I look like him?"

Derek rubs his chin. "No, thank God. I hate to be shallow, but if you looked like that I don't know that I'd be into you."

I roll my eyes. "Seriously, Derek."

"His face is like two millimeters wide."

"Yeah, I guess it's pretty hard to tell anything from this."

I flip to the back and look up Brad Roth next. Pretty much the same result. Tiny pictures and no real information.

"Look up your mom. Maybe there's a picture of her with someone named JJ?"

"How did you get so smart," I mutter, flipping to the back.

Charlotte Meyer is listed on six pages. On the first page there's a picture of her and a group of other people that includes my dad, Greg Jones. The next one has her standing with four other people, all men.

"Look here," I say, pointing to the caption. "'Graduate students Charlotte Meyer, Ben Stapleton, Jeff Hayes and Mark Hilton with Professor Stark.' Ben Stapleton isn't on our list."

Derek jots it down at the bottom of my growing list of suspects.

This is starting to feel like a very twisted game of Clue. I put my head in my hands and massage my scalp with my fingers. "I don't feel like we're getting anywhere."

Derek rubs circles on my back. "That's not true. We're pretty sure it's this JJ person, right? So all we have to do is track down just one person who knows who JJ is. We've only been at it for a couple of days—we'll get there."

"I hope so."

"How about that Liz woman? We have like three suspects on Facebook, let's just shoot them all messages and see which one gets back to us."

I stare at my list. Paul and Tobi both live in Cleveland. Maybe Derek was right. Maybe we should head up there. "Were you serious about going to Cleveland?"

"Sure." His laptop is open, and he's logged onto my Facebook page. He types like mad. "It's not even noon. I say we just go on up. We should be back here by dark."

"Let's do it then. I think we need a change of scenery, and it seems like fate that two of the people we need to talk to live up there."

He shuts his laptop and pulls me to my feet. "Maybe we can even check with Drew Carey's family while we're up there? Just in case."

I shove him. "Drew Carey is not my dad!"

My stomach is growling by the time we roll into Cleveland, so Derek hits a drive-through on the way to Tobi Nakamura's house. The burger is greasy and gross—and exactly what I needed. I only eat red meat when I'm upset. Guess my future has a lot of red meat in it.

Tobi lives in a nice neighborhood, the kind that's home to doctors and lawyers and other professionals. Maybe even Drew Carey's family. The houses aren't new, but they're well maintained and updated, and even the snow can't cover up the meticulous way these people have watched over their homes. Or probably more accurately, the people they've hired.

My heart beats like a drum as Derek and I walk up to her front door, but I don't know why exactly. She probably isn't even home; it's the middle of the afternoon on a Wednesday. I ring the doorbell and tap my toe on the icy welcome mate. A few seconds later, the door opens.

Except for a slight crinkle at the corner of her eyes, Tobi Nakamura looks exactly like she did in the pictures. "Can I help you?"

For a full ten seconds I don't speak. I really wasn't prepared for her to be home. She frowns, and her eyes go back and forth between the two of us. The look on her face has me even more tongue-tied. Derek clears his throat, and when I manage to rip my eyes away from Tobi, he nods. Right. I need to get down to business.

I take a deep breath and turn back to her. "My name is Kara Jones, and you don't know me and you're probably going to think I'm insane, but I think you went to Kent with my mom, Charlotte Meyer, and I just recently found out that my dad isn't my dad, and she's been lying to me for all these years, but she refuses to tell me who my real dad is, which is why I'm here trying to track down people who knew her when she was in college." It sounds like the longest run-on sentence in the history of the world, and if it wasn't for the fact that Tobi's eyes get bigger with each word I say, I'd have to wonder if she can even understand me. My heart pounds and my lungs burn. I pause to gather courage. "I was wondering if you had any idea who my real father might be."

Tobi steps back and pulls the door open wider. "Why don't you come inside?"

My heart jumps to my throat, and I start to shake. Does this mean she knows something? You'd think I'd be happier at the prospect instead of having this insane urge to run. Derek squeezes my hand. I'm so glad he's here! Without him, I never would have gotten this far.

Tobi's house is as immaculate and elegant as the neighborhood, and she fits in perfectly. She's wearing heels and a plum-colored suit, and her shoes click across the marble floors as she leads us through the house. My heart synchronizes with the sound, thumping so hard that I have trouble concentrating on anything else.

We end up in a living room. Tobi whips out her phone and motions toward the couch before typing away. "I have to send my partner a quick text to let her know I got held up."

I nod and lower myself to the couch. Derek puts his hand on my back. My entire body tingles, and I have to remind myself not to freak out. *Okay, Kara, you need to relax. Inhale. Exhale. Inhale. Stay calm.*

Tobi turns her phone off and sits in an armchair. Her eyes hold mine, and the tension in my body builds until it feels like my head is going to pop off. My throat tightens. If she doesn't say something soon I'm going to scream at her.

"This isn't really that much of a surprise, to be honest," she finally says.

Derek's mouth drops open, and my insides twist into a

tight ball.

I grip the arms of the chair. "You expected me? Did someone tell you I was coming?"

She rubs her temple. "No to both. I never would have expected Charlotte's daughter to show up at my door, but…" She takes a deep breath, like she's preparing to drop a bomb. "I thought your mom might have been seeing someone else, and then your parents broke up and it kind of confirmed my suspicions."

A million questions go through my mind, and I have a difficult time concentrating. Did my dad lie to me too? Is that why he isn't calling me back? What if he's known this whole time? Then I'll have no one left.

A part of me doesn't want to ask, but I *have* to know. "Did you ever mention your suspicions to my dad?"

"They broke up, so there didn't really seem to be much of a point. I hated to kick someone when they were already down."

My head nods on its own. He didn't lie to me. I only wish it made things better. "So what made you think my mom was seeing someone else?"

"The weeks leading up to your parents split up, Charlotte was very distant. She wasn't hanging out as much, and she seemed to need to study a lot more. I tried to tell myself she was just focusing on her degree. She was spending a lot of time with other people in her department and her professor. But it felt like more than that."

This is all great information, but it doesn't get me any closer to finding out who my father is. I mean, I already know my mom decided to whore it up.

"But you don't know who it was?" There's a slight edge to my voice, and I swallow. I need to keep it together.

Tobi shakes her head, and it feels like someone reached down my throat and squeezed my lungs. I try to swallow around the giant arm that's choking me, but it just makes my throat feel raw. Isn't there a single person my mom trusted enough to confide in? These were supposed to be her good friends, but they didn't even know her. Of course, I'm her daughter, and I guess I've never really known her either. It makes me wonder if my mom has ever allowed another person to get close to her.

"I wasn't that close to your mom—or anyone else for that matter. Back then I was kind of distancing myself from my own life. I hadn't fully accepted who I was. I'm not the best person to ask about other people's personal lives. I was kind of just a spectator."

So Grace was right about Tobi.

Derek scoots to the edge of the edge of his chair. "Did Charlotte ever mention anyone named JJ?"

Tobi sits up straighter. "JJ? That does sound familiar."

The arm dislodges itself from my throat, and I suck in a deep breath. Maybe there is hope after all! "Do you remember anything about him?"

Tobi shakes her head. "No, sorry. I wish I could be more helpful."

What is it with this JJ guy? Why doesn't anyone know who he was? It's creepy, actually. The way everyone seems to have heard of him, but no one ever met him. What was my mom trying to hide?

I sink back into my chair, but Derek pats my leg. "Where's that list?"

Oh yeah, the list. I guess it's worth a shot. I open the notebook and scan the list of names that aren't crossed out. There aren't many left.

"Do you have any idea where Brad Roth is?"

"Brad died a few years ago. Car accident."

"Great," I mumble. "Another dead end."

Derek tenses, and I have the urge to hit myself in the head. *Real smooth, Kara.*

"Sorry—that's not what I meant."

Derek nods but stares at his hands. Awesome. I'm hurting so I have to take everyone down with me.

Tobi glances at her phone. "I get it. Brad's not your dad anyway—he was gay."

"Oh." Well, that's another one I can cross off the list. "Do you know Jason Simpson or Ben Stapleton?"

She shakes her head. "Neither name sounds familiar."

I focus all my energy on scratching out Brad Roth. The tip of the pen digs into the paper as I run it back and forth, blotting away every millimeter of the name. The paper rips and Derek puts his hand on mine.

"It's okay," he whispers. "We'll figure it out."

The paper blurs, and I blink. When I look up, Tobi is frowning at me.

"I'm so sorry. I wish I could help you more."

Why is that how every one of these conversations ends? And why is it all these strangers want to help me find my father, but my own mom has no interest?

CHAPTER FIFTEEN

"I'm sorry," I say the second both car doors are shut. "I shouldn't have said that."

"Don't be." Derek starts the car but doesn't look at me for a few seconds. He takes a few deep breaths. "I knew what you meant, and anyway, it didn't have anything to do with my family."

"Still was a jerk thing to say."

He finally looks at me and grins, and my body melts into the seat. "Forget it. Let's go check out this other guy."

Paul Fitzgerald's house is in a less ostentatious neighborhood. The kind that would have kids riding bikes up and down the street in the summer, or running through sprinklers in front yards. We pass more than one snowman family, and for some reason, being here helps ease the tension. This reminds me of the neighborhood I grew up in. Solid middle-class. Happy families living happy lives. That's what I've always thought my life was. Do these people have skeletons in their closets too? Is there anyone on this street walking around carrying a secret big enough to rip a family apart? I can't imagine.

Derek pulls over in front of a brick house, and before he even has the car in park, I can tell no one is home. The windows are dark, and the driveway isn't plowed. There are no car tracks leading to the garage.

"Looks like he's gone," Derek mutters.

"Is there even any point in knocking?"

Derek looks over his shoulder. "The neighbor is out shoveling his driveway. Maybe he knows something?"

I glance out the back window, craning my neck so I can see. The guy has to be in his seventies. "You think he'll tell us whippersnappers?"

Derek's dimple gets deeper. "It's worth a shot. Stay here and I'll go find out."

He's out the door before I can protest. I undo my belt and spin around in my seat, so I can watch him through the back window. Derek jumps over a few snow drifts, slipping once and almost falling.

When he stops in front of the man, the old guy stiffens. Derek starts talking and waving his hands around, pointing to Paul's house, and the man relaxes. It's hard to tell from here, but it looks like he might even be smiling. I guess Derek's charm works on old men, too.

He runs back—more like slides—after only a few minutes. When he hops into the car he shivers. "Paul Fitzgerald and his family are on vacation. They'll be home tomorrow morning." He puts the car in drive and grins. "How do you feel about getting a hotel?"

My stomach twists and my heart skips a beat, and my first instinct is to shout with joy. I swallow and say as calmly as I can manage, "We don't have anything with us."

"We can stop somewhere and grab some shampoo and stuff, so we don't smell tomorrow. Maybe get you a new lacy thong." He wiggles his eyebrows.

I laugh even though my heart is beating faster than a race horse. "Or I could just go without."

His hands tighten on the steering wheel, and he clears his throat. "I'm a big fan of that idea."

We luck out. There's a drug store right across the street

from the Hampton Inn. We grab a couple toothbrushes, some toothpaste, and deodorant. I get some shampoo—the hotel stuff is always crap—and a razor. Hairy legs and armpits are so *not* sexy. When I pass the condoms, I stop. Derek is on the other side of the store loading up on Gatorade, like he's worried hydration might be a problem. Is he thinking the same thing as me? On impulse I grab a box. Doesn't hurt to be prepared. There's no law that says we *have* to use them just because I buy them…

"You ready?" Derek calls.

I shove the box in my basket and nod, but as I walk toward him, I cover it up with the shampoo and razors. The thought of him seeing them makes my stomach churn. In the heat of the moment sex sounds like a fantastic idea, but right now I'm freaking out. It's been almost two years, and I can't say I ever really enjoyed it that much. Bill was an ass and selfish, and sex with him was nothing more than just a few minutes of him wiggling around on top of me.

Derek puts his stuff down in front of the cashier. "My treat." He tilts his head toward the counter as he pulls out his wallet.

"No, I got this." There's no possible way for me to hide these condoms with him standing right next to me. Why don't they have more than one cashier working?

Derek puts his wallet on the counter. "Kara, it's no big deal."

Before I can stop him, he grabs the shampoo out. His eyes get big, and he glances up at me. Then he clears his throat, and his face relaxes. He calmly unloads the basket without another word, but the whole time my face is on fire. I escape by taking the basket back to the pile by the front door.

He's next to me before my heart rate has a chance to return to normal. His hand rests on my lower back as he leads me to the door. Even through my jacket and sweater his touch burns my skin.

He doesn't talk again until we're in the car, and he hands me the bags so he can drive. "I didn't suggest a hotel so you'd sleep with me."

I force out a tight laugh. "I'm pretty sure we've already slept together a few times."

He grins, but his eyes are on the road. We're at a light. All we have to do is cross the street, and we'll be in the hotel parking lot. My leg shakes.

"That's not what I meant."

"I know what you meant. Buying them doesn't obligate us to use them. You know, better safe than sorry."

The light turns green. We cross the street and pull into the parking lot. My heart pounds. I grip the bag and the plastic crinkling in my hands is so loud it drowns out every other noise.

Derek puts the car in park and studies my face. His eyes go down to my hands—still gripping the bag. "I wouldn't want you to be sorry."

Now my face is really on fire. "Let's just check in and grab some dinner. I'm starving."

It's not really true. At the moment, my stomach feels like it's inside out and the burger I ate earlier is desperate to escape, but I want to get out of this car. My leg is shaking so bad that the bag vibrates. Derek frowns, but he doesn't argue, and the second I step outside I exhale. Steam rises in front of me and I concentrate on watching it drift into the sky. Just last night I was more than ready to have sex with Derek. Why am I so nervous now?

We check in, head up to the room—which has one bed—and order pizza. Derek lays back on the bed and starts flipping through the pay-per-view movies. I try to relax. The condoms are still in the bag, and he hasn't brought it up again, but it's all I can think about.

"What are you thinking?" Derek says, making me jump.

My heart pounds as I think about how to answer that question. Ripping your clothes off? Running away?

"Comedy or action? I don't think I'm in the mood for a

drama."

Oh! He's talking about the movie. "Comedy."

"That's what I was thinking too."

We eat pizza and watch a stupid movie about a single girl who gets set up on a bunch of blind dates by her married friends. It's typical Hollywood crap—she manages to set her first date on fire, and her second date is with a guy she dumped only a month earlier—but it's entertaining. By the time the credits roll I'm relaxed again.

"Now what?" Derek asks. "We could get another movie. They have a few adult selections too."

"So typical. I knew you were luring me up here to take advantage of me."

"I just don't like wasting money." I frown, and he motions toward the bag. "I paid for the condoms. Not using them is wasting money."

"Right. Well, we could figure out other ways to use them. Water balloon fight?"

He chuckles. "Unless we use them for their intended purpose, I'm pretty sure it's still a waste."

My heart pounds and I scoot closer to him until there are only a few inches of space between us. "Then I guess we'll just have to use them the right way."

He kisses me, soft and gentle, then pushes me onto my back. His hands run down my body until he reaches my stomach. But he doesn't move for a few seconds, and he stops kissing me.

"I was serious, Kara. I don't want you to be sorry."

"I won't be."

Derek looks uncertain. I want him to know I'm serious, so I pull my shirt over my head and toss it to the ground. He pushes my bra strap down and kisses my neck, then my shoulder, caressing every inch of my skin until he reaches the top of my bra. I reach up to undo the clasp, but he beats me to it. He pulls it aside, smiles, and sits back. His eyes travel over me like he's looking at a priceless work of art.

When he brings his mouth back to mine, I pull his shirt over his head and go for the button on his pants.

"I should grab a condom," he says against my mouth, but he doesn't get up.

His kiss grows deeper, and he fumbles with my jeans as I trace his tongue with mine. I pull him close and kiss him hungrily, but it isn't close enough. I've never felt like this before. Never wanted something so bad. The button on his pants comes undone, and I slowly pull the zipper down.

He groans when my fingers slip inside, and pulls away. "Condom."

He hops off the bed, and I take the opportunity to pull my pants off. My skin is moist with sweat, and my heart is pounding. I can't get my clothes off fast enough. Derek must be thinking the same thing, because he wiggles out of his pants while ripping the box open. Desire and lust and need swirl around in my stomach and between my legs when he heads back, clutching a condom and wearing nothing but his boxer briefs.

I'm in a lacy thong.

He puts the condom on the bedside table before hooking his fingers in my thong and slowly pulling it down. I raise my hips, allowing him easier access. Once it's off, he tosses it to the floor and climbs onto the bed. His mouth covers mine, his hands moving over my body. He pulls my leg up over his hip, and his body moves against me. There's a slight ache in my side with every move, but it isn't bad enough to make me want to stop. Only his boxer briefs separate us. The longer we kiss and the more he touches me, the more I want them gone.

I reach for the condom. My hands shake as I try to rip the package open, but it isn't working. Dammit! Do you have to have a key to get into these things or what?

Derek takes it out of my hand, and I lean back, panting.

He smiles at me. "Is this like opening a jar?"

"Shut up and open the damn thing."

His smile widens.

My phone dings and I glance toward it out of habit. The little text alert is like a cold shower. It's Dad.

When I sit up, Derek frowns.

"I'm sorry." I reach for my phone. "It's from my dad. I haven't heard from him since I got back from the hospital."

He's still holding the unopened condom. I bite my lip and look back and forth between the condom and the phone. My body screams at me to put the phone down—the text will be there in the morning—but my heart begs me to read it. My heart wins.

There's a text from my mom too, but I deal with my dad first.

Dad: *Kara—I'm so sorry. My phone has been off. I just couldn't talk to anyone right now. I still love you too, honey, and of course I want to see you. Give me a call when you get back in town.*

Tears fill my eyes, and Derek sits up. "Hey, it's okay." He pulls me against him, and I lay my head on his bare chest.

"I'm just so glad to finally hear from him. The past few days I've been feeling so abandoned. If it hadn't been for you, I would have gone insane." I look up at him.

He kisses my forehead, and it's quite possibly the sweetest gesture I've ever experienced. "I'm glad I could be here. And this has been good for me. I've been pretty secluded the past nine months."

I wipe my eyes with the back of my hand and pull up the text from my mom. "I guess we've been good for each other."

"Yeah," he says.

Mom: *Checking in. I want to know when you'll be home.*

She's getting impatient. Maybe I should tell her where I am. Maybe if she knows how serious I am about finding my father, she'll decide to tell me who it is.

Kara: *Derek and I drove up to Kent.*

I toss the phone on the bed and head to the bathroom

to get a tissue. Derek's his eyes follow me across the room, soaking in every move I make.

When I come back, he holds the condom up. I guess my text didn't kill the mood for him.

"If I remember correctly you were trying to get this open?"

I smile and push him onto his back and climb on top, so I'm straddling him. His smile fades when I take the condom away. He runs his hands up my body, starting at my thighs and working his way up until he's cupping both of my breasts. I lean down and kiss him, lightly tracing my tongue over his lips as I rip the condom open.

My phone rings and I sit up. It's right next to my knee. I reach for it and Derek curses. I'm only planning to put it on the night stand until I see that it's my mom. Crap. What if she's calling to tell me who my dad is? Then all this can be over, and I can focus on Derek and not have to worry about all this private investigator bullshit.

"It will just take a second," I say, hitting the answer button. "Mom?"

"Kara, how could you do this?" Her voice is high and shaky.

I guess she hasn't changed her mind. "Look, you may not understand why I need to do this, but I'm not going to change my mind. I want to know where I came from. It doesn't have to be the huge deal that you're making it into."

"Kara, I am *begging* you. Forget about all this and come home. There are some things in life that you don't need to know. Greg Jones is your dad. I never told you differently because that's the way I wanted it to be."

I'm still straddling Derek, and he's frozen under me. My body shakes and my chest tightens again. "Just because you want it to be that way doesn't mean it's real."

"Kara…" Her voice shakes with desperation.

I roll off Derek and move so my back is to him. I need to focus on my mom. There has to be something I can say to make her understand. "You have to know me well enough to realize that I'm not going to just drop this whole thing. Save us both some trouble and just tell me."

"And you have to know me well enough to understand that if I refuse to tell you there has to be a really good reason."

She's never going to give in. I rest my forehead against the wall and close my eyes. "I'm hanging up now. Don't call me back unless you decide you want to be honest with me. I can't take any more lies, Mom. It's killing me."

I press end before she can say anything else. My hand falls to my side, and the phone drops to the floor, but I don't move. My forehead is still pressed against the wall when Derek comes up behind me. He runs his hand across my back, but unlike a few minutes ago there's nothing sexual about it. My body is numb. All the desire I felt has disappeared.

Derek turns me around, and I press my cheek against his chest. Neither one of us talks.

CHAPTER SIXTEEN

When I come out of the bathroom, showered and dressed, Derek is laying across the bed with his laptop open in front of him. I can't help feeling a little guilty about last night. Things have to be turning blue by this point.

"You didn't check your Facebook page yesterday did you?"

"No. I don't check it much. Why?"

"You have two messages."

It takes me a minute to remember what he's talking about. Liz Winston! "I forgot all about that. Either one from the Liz we're looking for?"

Derek opens the first one, and I read it over his shoulder. Nope, not the Liz Winston that used to be Liz Marcum and went to Kent with my mom.

"Check the second one."

Derek opens the second message. "Bingo."

I lean closer and my heart goes from thumping excitedly to dropping to the floor in two seconds. "Too bad she doesn't know anything." I throw myself onto the bed next Derek. "Why can't my mom just be reasonable?"

Derek shuts the computer and pushes it aside. He runs his fingers through my hair, brushing it off my forehead, then twisting it around two digits. "I'm sorry." He presses his lips against mine. It's soft and brief, but it still makes me shiver.

I run my hand through his brown hair, and it drops down over his eyebrow. "I'm sorry about last night."

"You don't need to be sorry."

"But I am."

Derek rolls over and looks at the clock. "We need to be back in Kent by three to meet with Dr. Hilton. It's almost eleven now, and we'll probably want to grab lunch. We should get going."

I groan, but only inwardly. Last night was the perfect opportunity, and I *really* wanted to. But it's not the end of the world. It's not like we aren't going to have another opportunity.

I push myself off the bed and hop to my feet. "Okay, let's move out then."

When we pull up in front of Paul's house, the driveway has been cleared, and the curtains are open.

"Guess they made it back." I hop out of the car. "Hopefully, he can tell us something."

Paul Fitzgerald is almost completely bald. He smiles when he answers the door, and his brown eyes look pretty friendly, so I dive right in. I stick with my story about trying to reunite my mom with a long lost love.

He pushes the door open wider and scratches his scalp. "I remember your mom, but we never dated. She and I worked together at the campus bookstore. She was pretty focused on academics to be honest. I even remember her spending extra time with her professor. Things seemed a little tough for her for a bit, though. I remember she and your dad broke up, then she got pretty sick. Missed a lot of work. When she came back she wasn't the same. Thought she'd be happy, you know? She and Greg ran off and got married, then everyone found out she was pregnant." He shrugs. "But she was just a different person. Skittish. It's hard to explain."

My stomach tightens and an odd sense of dread comes over me, but I have no clue why. Derek gives me a reassuring squeeze. I'm glad his arm is around me because it's freezing outside.

Paul taps his finger against his lips a few times. "You know who you might try though, is Amy Ceccoli. Amy worked with us and I know she and your mom were pretty close."

Okay, another name. But I can't let myself get too excited. Just because this guy thinks Amy might know something doesn't necessarily mean she will. It could be another dead end. "Do you know where we might be able to find her?" A gust of wind sweeps across the yard. It would be nice if he'd ask us to come inside like Tobi did.

Paul leans against the doorframe. Guess he isn't going to let us in. "I'm not positive. But I did run into her a few years ago, and she was still going by her maiden name then—can't be too hard to track her down. It's not like her name is Smith or anything."

I sigh but pull my notebook out anyway. He has a point, but I'm still starting to feel like we're running around in circles. My fingers are like icicles as I pull the cap off my pen. "Can you tell me how to spell it?"

Paul spells it out and we ask him about the other people on our list. He doesn't know a thing, or at least doesn't remember. Oh well, we got the name of one more person to contact. If we can find her.

We grab a quick lunch, and we're in the car and headed back to Kent by a quarter after one—that should give us plenty of time to make it to AlphaMicron. I spend the drive on my phone, searching for Amy Ceccoli.

"Finding anything?" Derek asks.

"There are a few suspects, but it would be easier if we could check on a computer. This one looks pretty likely." I tap the screen. "She lives in Germany, though."

"We'll give it a look when we get back to Dex's."

We roll into AlphaMicron's parking lot at two forty. The same woman is behind the desk, and once again she acts like she's never seen us before. Derek and I sit in the uncomfortable waiting room. I keep a close eye on the clock while we Google Amy Ceccoli.

Today I don't wait. At ten after three I go back to the receptionist.

I'm not the least bit surprised when she says, "I'm afraid that Dr. Hilton isn't going to be able to meet with you today. Would you like to reschedule for tomorrow?"

What's the deal with this place? "Yes," I say, through gritted teeth.

We reschedule for noon the following day, but I don't have a lot of confidence that we're going to get in to see Dr. Hilton then or any other time. He seems to be avoiding us. Or maybe this chick isn't even telling him we're here. She seems to have a personal vendetta against me.

Derek and I stop in the middle of the parking lot, and he rubs the back of my neck. "So maybe this JJ person doesn't have anything to do with this. Maybe Mark Hilton is your dad."

Despite the cold air, the sun is bright and warm. It feels nice on my face. Like my own personal heater.

I lean into Derek's fingers when they touch a sore spot. "Yeah, I was thinking the same thing. If he isn't, it's strange that he keeps blowing us off."

Derek stops rubbing my neck and grabs my hand, pulling me toward the car. "We can Google him too. See if we can come up with a home address."

I'd tell Derek he's a genius, but I'm pretty sure he already knows.

"You're back!" Dex beams when he opens the door.

"Good. We're having a party tonight."

"Thank God." I drop onto the futon without even taking off my jacket. "I need a drink."

Dex adjusts his sweater vest. He *has* to be gay. "You didn't find anything?"

Derek opens the computer and sits down next to me. I lean my head against his shoulder. "We got a little more information, but I still have no idea who my father is. This whole process is infuriating."

"We do have leads though," Derek says. "Look here." He points to the screen where Amy Ceccoli's name is listed under the board of directors for some German company. Then he flips to another window and pulls up a LinkedIn page for Amy Ceccoli. It lists the same work information and her alma mater as Kent State University. "I'd say that's her."

I sit up and grab Derek's arm. Could it really have been that easy to find this woman? "It even has her work number!"

Derek points to the screen. "But she lives in Germany, that's what? Five hours later?"

"Six," Dex says. I raise an eyebrow at him, and he shrugs. "My dad's in the Air Force, we lived there for a few years before he got stationed at Wright-Patt." His eyes are focused on my chest. Not gay? I can't figure this guy out.

It's almost four here.

"Crap. That means we can't call tonight." That only leaves one thing to do. "Let's just get drunk."

Derek and Dex started shotgunning beers at five—not gay. Now it's a little after seven, and they are both hammered. Not that I can complain, I'm three beers in myself and feeling pretty good. Or is it four?

More people trickle in, and we order pizza. I'm too

depressed to really care that Derek and I had the same thing for dinner last night. All I want to do is get drunk and forget about my mom.

Most of the people I recognize from the first party—Steph included—and right away Mitch starts in on who my dad might be. I'm not really in the mood, but I let it go and drink more. Maybe he can get me to laugh about the depressing state my life has become.

Steph's appearance has done something to Derek. He had his arm around me before she showed up, but now that she's here he can't seem to stop touching me. Not all of it in places appropriate for public viewing. I'm on his lap, listening to Mitch go through his Drew Carey theory. Derek traces a line up the side of my leg to my arm and back down. His fingers stray a little too close to my inner thigh, then dangerously close to my breast. He's driving me wild. If Steph wasn't sitting here, or if I were at all into PDA, I would kiss him. Or maybe if I was drunker… I finish off my beer. Four down. Or five?

"So what's your mom's reason for not telling you exactly?" Debbie asks. She's glued to Mitch's side, but I can't tell if the feeling is mutual. Doesn't seem like it. Mitch has been very close to Derek and me the whole night. His eyes follow the progress of Derek's hand as it moves up and down my body.

"She just keeps saying sometimes a lie is better than the truth. Whatever that means."

Mitch elbows Debbie and her face lights up. Nope, not an established thing yet. Maybe never. I get the feeling she's in the friend zone.

"Oooh…" He stretches the word out like something mysterious has happened. "Another chapter in the Kent University Curse maybe?"

I blink and try to focus on Mitch's words despite Derek's fingers moving up my inner thigh. Does he have any idea what he's doing to me? "A curse? Seriously?"

Debbie and Mitch nod enthusiastically, but Steph's the

one who answers. "The university has had some bad luck over the years." Her voice is flat, and her eyes are trained on Derek's hand. "Murder and suicide—all that fun stuff."

I can't meet her eyes directly. Not with Derek's fingers moving over my skin and my insides burning like I'm sitting in the middle of a forest fire.

I focus on Debbie. "Like what?"

She waves her hand in the air and when it comes down it lands on Mitch's leg. He looks at it and smirks, but doesn't push it away. "I'm sure you've heard of the Kent State massacre."

It sounds familiar. Something that happened in the '60s or '70s, I think. "Did that have something to do with Vietnam?"

Dex flops down next to Steph, spilling her beer. He doesn't seem to notice that, or the glare she gives him. "Yup. The National Guard opened fire on protestors. Like thirty people were killed."

"Four," she snaps. She shakes her hand in his face and a few drops of beer land on his glasses. "Four were killed and a few more wounded."

I nod and the room spins a little. My face and neck are hot. Is it from the alcohol or Derek's hand? Which is now under my sweater, stroking my spine and making every nerve in my body buzz with excitement. "What else happened?" My voice is as shaky as my body. He has to know he's driving me wild.

"A few suicides here and there—although that might be common," Debbie says. "Maybe that happens at all schools? You know, from the pressure of college." She shrugs and starts moving her hand on Mitch's leg. Mitch clears his throat and leans back like he's just going to enjoy the ride.

Suicides? I have no idea if it's common, so I just shrug. My tongue is stuck to the roof of my mouth, and every muscle in my body has turned to mush. With the way Derek is stroking my bare skin, I am quickly losing interest in this conversation.

Mitch grins even bigger than before. "Then there was that murder-suicide last year. Some crazy love triangle. A guy killed his ex-girlfriend, and her new boyfriend then shot himself."

Why does Mitch look so excited? It isn't from Debbie's hand, that's for sure. He's smiling like he's talking about a celebrity visiting the school. My mind flashes to the Drew Carey theory, and I almost laugh. Everything but Derek's hand is fuzzy.

"Then there were all those murders back in like mid-nineties." Dex's words are slurred, but he has my attention back. Well half. The other half is still focused on Derek's hand. I'm pretty sure he's working at undoing my bra. Yup. There it goes.

I inhale and try to pay attention to what the others are saying. Derek's hand goes up my back to my shoulder. He moves my hair aside with his nose, and his lips touch my neck. I swallow when his hand moves back down, then up to my waist, grazing the side of my breast.

"He killed, like, ten women before they found him," Debbie says. Her brown eyes are twice as big as they were a moment ago, and her hand has stopped moving on Mitch's leg. He's staring at it like his puppy died. Men.

"It was awful," some blonde girl I don't know says. I'm pretty sure she's the one who looked Drew Carey up on her phone the other night. "He tortured those poor women."

"When they arrested Professor Stark everyone was in shock. He was really popular with the students," Steph says.

Derek's hand stops moving, and I snap to attention. What did she say?

"Who?" Derek asks.

"Professor Stark." Steph stares at Derek, and her blue eyes are colder than Alaska in January.

Professor Stark. The name means something to me,

and it takes a few seconds to remember why. That's the professor my mom had her picture taken with in the yearbook. Is that why Derek is so still, or is it because Steph is staring at us?

"Then there was another shooting before that. Early nineties," Mitch says. "Some guy had killed a janitor a few months before and then opened fire on campus. He shot one girl before police took him out, but she survived." Debbie's hand is once again caressing his leg, and Mitch is lounging in the chair like he's on vacation. I have a feeling he's getting laid tonight.

"Nice school you chose," Derek says dryly, taking a drink. His hand starts moving on my back again.

Dex shoots him a lopsided grin and raises his beer can. "Part of the appeal. I like someone with a dark past." Was it my imagination, or did he look at me when he said that? Maybe he isn't gay…

Derek's hand erases every thought from my mind when it slides around and cups my breast completely. I lean back against him and close my eyes, pressing my face in the nape of his neck. Who cares if Steph is watching? I don't want him to stop.

"Damn," he says against my ear "We should have stayed at the hotel another night."

"Hmmm," I murmur.

"Derek," Dex says, clearing his throat.

My eyes fly open. He's grinning from ear to ear, but other than Steph, he's the only one really paying attention to us. Everyone else is too busy drinking. Derek's hand slips around to my back, and I sit up. I should probably be embarrassed, but I'm not.

"How's the graphic novel coming?" Dex asks.

CHAPTER SEVENTEEN

I open my eyes, then squint and cover my head. Why don't guys think to buy curtains? Why would anyone want this much light in their apartment this early in the morning?

Derek rolls over and his hand moves under my shirt and traces its way up my spine.

"I'm too hung over," I moan into the pillow.

"You didn't seem to mind last night."

"Last night my head didn't pound and my mouth didn't taste like something took a dump in it."

Derek chuckles, and his hand leaves my back. "That's hot."

"I'm not trying to turn you on." I roll over even though it hurts, and pry my eyes back open. Why *is* it so bright in here? "What time is it?"

Derek grabs his phone, then bolts upright. "Shit. It's after eleven. We're supposed to be at AlphaMicron by noon."

I don't move a muscle. "What's the point? It's not like Dr. Hilton is actually going to see us."

Derek grabs my arm and pulls me up. "Come on. You'll be mad at yourself later if we don't do this. It's Friday morning, this is our last chance before the weekend."

He's right, dammit. "Do I have time for a cold shower?"

"As long as it isn't longer than five minutes."

The lobby of AlphaMicron is different than usual. Cheerful music fills the room, and the blonde with the severe hairstyle isn't sitting behind the desk. Instead, there's a woman whose brown hair dances around her shoulders every time she moves. She bops her head to the music like it's on a top '40s station instead of the instrumental crap you usually hear in elevators.

Her shirt is yellow, and her smile is so bright it's like looking at the sun. "Hello! You must be the noon appointment with Dr. Hilton?"

"Um…yes." My head hurts and the constant bopping she's doing makes me want to puke.

"Excellent! Take a seat and I'll let him know you're here." She motions to the chairs and types at the computer. I guess they don't do phones here.

"That's weird," Derek says.

"No kidding. You think we'll actually get to see him today? Maybe that blonde chick was just being a nasty bitch."

"Anything's possible."

Five minutes later I almost jump out of my snow boots when the receptionist's voice echoes through the room. "Ms. Jones? Mr. Miller? Dr. Hilton is available to see you now."

I look at Derek, and he shrugs.

She leads us through the double doors and down a long hallway. We go right at the end then head down another seemingly endless hall. We pass a few glass windows that reveal labs and a lot of closed doors—all unmarked— before turning into an open doorway. A man in his forties with dusty brown hair stands with his back to us. When he turns to face us, he smiles.

"This is your noon appointment, Dr. Hilton," the receptionist practically sings.

The doctor nods, and the receptionist is still bopping her head when she walks out the door. I cross my arms over my chest and wait for the doctor to say he's too busy to see us right now, but he takes a seat at the desk and motions toward the chairs.

"Please, sit down."

Okay, now this is really crazy.

The second Derek and I sit the doctor smiles. "What can I do for you? It seems you've been trying to see me the past few days, and you keep coming back, so it must be important."

"Is there a reason you were blowing us off?" I have to know what I'm dealing with before I go any further. This whole thing has been too crazy.

He leans back and puts his hands behind his head. "Not avoiding. We had a little mishap in one of the labs a few days ago, and I'm afraid I was running around like crazy trying to clean up the mess and deal with internal stuff. Normally, I would never blow off an appointment."

Is he telling the truth? He looks pretty relaxed, and he doesn't seem upset that we're here. I guess I'll just have to ask my questions and decide. So, I go through the whole thing with my mom again, and when I mention who she is he drops his hands and sits forward, but he's still smiling.

"I thought you looked familiar—you look just like Charlotte."

Okay, so he's admitting that he knows her. That's a good sign. "Were the two of you ever romantically involved?"

He shakes his head and sits back. "Nope. I asked her out, but she wasn't interested in me."

There goes another one. Great. There's a pit in my stomach that gets bigger with each dead end. At the moment, it feels like the Grand Canyon. I might as well ask my questions and get it over with. "Do you remember her ever mentioning someone named JJ?"

Dr. Hilton nods. "Oh yeah. She was dating your dad, but they broke up and she stopped coming around. When I called her to ask her out she told me she was seeing someone named JJ. No idea who it was."

Of course not. This JJ person is a phantom. Maybe he's imaginary.

I slump back in my chair as Derek leans forward. "I just want to get this out there because the fact that you wouldn't see us the last two days is pretty suspicious—"

Dr. Hilton's smile fades. "I told you why."

Derek shakes his head. "Are you Kara's real father?"

The doctor's eyebrows shoot up, and he looks at me. "No wonder you were suspicious about the meetings. No, I'm sorry, but I never had sex with Charlotte Meyer."

I get to my feet. I've had enough of this. My head hurts and my stomach aches and all I want to do is curl up in a ball and sleep. At this point, I have a hard time even caring. "Thank you for your time, Dr. Hilton."

I make it to the car before Derek grabs my arm and spins me around. "What are you doing? We didn't even ask about the other people on our list."

"Who cares?" I throw my hands in the air. "This whole thing is pointless, Derek. My mom should be telling me this stuff. My dad should be talking to me. A couple weeks ago I had this perfect family—two parents who loved each other and were still married. And now I have nothing." Tears stream down my cheeks and my shoulders shake, but I can't stop. I've managed to keep it together for so long, but it's all too much right now. "Everything went from being perfect to total shit in the blink of an eye, and I don't know how to handle it."

Derek puts his hands on my shoulders. "Don't you

think I understand?"

My breaths come out in little hiccups, and I want to tell him I'm sorry. That I know I'm being selfish and unreasonable, and my drama is nothing compared to his, but I can't get the words out. Whenever I open my mouth all I can do is gasp for air.

He hugs me to him, running his hand over my head and down my back, and I squeeze my eyes shut. "It's okay," he whispers. "We'll figure all this out. But even if we don't I'll be here. I'm not going anywhere."

He kisses the top of my head then my temple, and I turn my face up and his mouth finds mine. He presses my back against the car and kisses me harder, forcing my lips apart as he pushes his body against mine. The fire inside me never really died out, and the smoldering coals in my belly ignite. If I didn't know better, I'd think we were standing in the middle of the Mojave Desert.

"Derek," I say against his lips. "Take me back to Dex's."

My blood simmers for the entire thirteen minutes that it takes to get back to Dex's apartment. Thank God it's close and Dex has class. The second we're inside, I rip Derek's jacket off. He does the same to me, and we make our way through the apartment, kissing as we undress. I'm already down to just my pants when he pushes me onto the bed. His lips never leave mine. He unbuttons my jeans, and then he's kissing his way down my body, pulling my pants off as he goes. My eyes close and electricity moves through me when his lips go lower. The second he has my pants off, I pull him back up and work at getting his undone.

I wrap my fingers through the belt loops and tug his jeans down. "Condoms."

He hops off the bed and dashes across the room,

pulling his jeans the rest of the way off. The package is already open by the time he's back. I yank his boxer briefs down and my heart pounds when he slides the condom on.

Derek balances himself above me for a few seconds, and his brown eyes search mine. "You're sure?"

"Right now, you are the only thing in my life that I'm sure about."

The corner of his mouth twitches. Then he lowers his body against mine and slides inside. I squeeze my eyes shut and wrap my legs around his waist. His lips work their way up my neck while his body rocks against mine. It's nothing like it was with Bill, nothing like I've ever experienced before. Derek is gentle and loving, and our bodies fit so perfectly together that at this moment I'm positive he was made for me.

His mouth moves to my ear, and his breath tickles my skin. "I never expected to fall in love with you."

My body explodes and an electric current shoots through my veins. Between my gasps, I think I whisper, "I love you too."

Derek's fingers trace up and down my arm. "We missed our chance to call Amy Ceccoli."

I wrap the sheet tighter around me and look at the clock. It's after two: eight in Germany. "Crap."

"You sorry?"

I turn so I can see his face. "You mean about missing the chance to call Amy or the sex?"

"Both, I guess."

"I am sorry we missed the chance to call Amy. The sex—I'll only be sorry if we don't ever do it again."

The smile that spreads across his face sends my heart into overdrive. I let go of the sheet and sweep my fingers through his hair. I'm running my nails down his spine when the front door opens.

"Oh shit, sorry," comes a voice from behind us.

Derek pulls back, and we both look toward the door where Dex stands with a big smile on his face. I grab for the sheet, so I can cover my naked body and don't miss the fact that Dex tries to sneak a peek. Not gay? There are a few other people behind him, and they all look just as amused as Dex.

Derek rolls off the bed, grabs his jeans and pulls them on in one swift move. How is he always so smooth? "Sorry, man," he says with a grin.

I bundle up the sheet and wrap it around my body, then roll off the bed, almost falling in the process. "I'm gonna throw some clothes on," I mutter, sweeping my clothes up as I go.

"This might be yours," Dex says.

I turn round to see him grin and hold my red thong in the air. My cheeks get hotter than the sun.

Derek rips it out of his hand and tosses it to me, and I run from the room before my face bursts into flames. That wasn't exactly how I wanted my first time with Derek to go. Well, not the sex—that was perfect. The interruption though…not so much.

When I go back to the living room Derek is still shirtless, but he has a beer in his hand. Dex and the other people with him are all lounging around the living room, drinking too. Now that I get a better look, I recognize them from last night.

Dex looks up when I walk out. "You should call her anyway."

I stop walking. "What?"

"The German chick," he says. "It could be a cell phone number, you never know."

"She isn't German." I sit on the arm of the chair next to Derek. "She just lives there."

"Whatever. I still think you should give it a try."

Derek rubs my knee. "He has a point."

I guess he does. It's not going to hurt to just dial the number. If the place is closed, I'll get a message; but if it's her cell, she might answer.

"It's worth a shot." I pull out my notebook so I can look the number up. When I hit send, everyone in the room stares at me. It clicks a few times then starts to ring, and I hold my breath.

It picks up after the third ring and a musical voice says, "Hallo-I mean, hello?"

I swallow. "Is this Amy Ceccoli?"

"Yes is it."

"Hi, my name is Kara Jones. I think you used to work with my mom in Kent, Ohio—Charlotte Meyer."

"Oh. Yes, yes I did." She pauses, and I open my mouth to go into my spiel, but before I can say anything else she says, "It's been a long time. How is your mother?"

I need space, so I stand up and cross the room. "Good. Um… Look, Paul Fitzgerald gave me your name. He said you and my mom used to be pretty close."

She coughs or clears her throat quietly. "Yes we were. We were very good friends, actually. Unfortunately, we had a bit of a falling out and…Well, you know how that stuff goes."

"What did you fight about?" My heart pounds and everyone in the room is glued to my every word. I try not to focus on the eyes following me as I pace back and forth, but it isn't easy.

"Um…just silly stuff." She laughs, but it sounds forced. She's hiding something for sure.

I need to just lay it all out there; it's the only way. "Look, Amy, I recently found out that my dad—Greg Jones—isn't really my dad. My mom refuses to tell me who it is, but if there's anything you can tell me that might help, I'd really appreciate it."

Amy sighs. It's long and drawn-out, and it makes every muscle in my body tighten. "I do know who your father is, Kara. I'm the only person that knew other than your mom."

I stop pacing and turn my back to the people staring at me. Their eyes burn into me, so I squeeze mine shut like I can somehow block them out. I take three deep breaths. "Will you tell me?"

Amy sighs again and mutters something in German. Judging by the tone, I'd guess she's cussing. "Your mother doesn't want to tell you for a reason, Kara. Are you sure this is something you need to know?"

My heart pounds so hard the beat pulses through my entire body. My legs turn to rubber and I have to lean against the wall for support. Someone touches my back— Derek, I'm sure—but I can't move. I can't do anything but whisper, "Yes."

"Your mother was having an affair with her professor, Kara." I try to squeeze my eyes tighter. Something in my head screams at me to interrupt her, to stop her from talking before she says the next words. "Professor Jonathon Stark to be exact. He was arrested just a week after she found out she was pregnant with you. Charged with the kidnapping and murder of ten women."

CHAPTER EIGHTEEN

The world spins, and my legs give out. Derek tries to hold me up, but it doesn't work, and I crash to the floor. Somehow I manage to keep the phone to my ear.

"No." This can't be happening. It's like a nightmare or horrible movie.

I rub my head like it will somehow turn back time.

"I'm sorry," Amy says. "Maybe I shouldn't have told you, I don't know. Your mom had already told me she was pregnant when JJ got arrested."

I whimper, and Derek moves closer. He rubs my arm. "JJ?"

"That was her nickname for him. Jonathon Jacob Stark—JJ."

I never learned his first name. Maybe if I had I would have suspected, and then I could have stopped this crazy search before learning the truth. Would that be better? Never knowing? I'm not sure. I'm not sure about anything right now. My brain is fuzzy, and everything seems out of focus. How did my mom go from JJ to my dad, and what does it all mean?

"So she went back to my dad after JJ got arrested?"

I think I'm talking to myself, trying to piece it all together in my head, but Amy answers anyway. "Yes. I told her to tell Greg the truth. I was certain your father would have taken her back regardless, but she didn't want anyone to know. I think she secretly hoped that you'd turn out to be Greg's baby anyway. There was a little bit of an overlap in the relationships."

My head hurts. I don't want to talk to this woman anymore. I hand the phone to Derek and lay my head against the wall, closing my eyes, so I don't have to face the other people in this room. I don't want them to know. My dad isn't Drew Carey or the governor or even the prince of a small country. He's a psychotic serial killer who tortured women. That's where I come from.

Mom was right. Sometimes a lie is better than the truth.

"This is Kara's boyfriend," Derek says. Is he my boyfriend? I guess he is. "She's a little upset right now. Yes. Yes. Yes."

Why does he keep saying that? I crack one eye. He's sitting next to me, nodding with the phone held to his ear.

"I understand. Thanks for all your help. She's,"— he glances at me —"in shock right now, but I think she'll be glad you told her. Eventually."

I close my eyes again. Will I? Is there any way to ever be happy to know this? No. It's impossible. Right now, I'd trade both my legs to erase the last few weeks from my mind. If only I hadn't been in that accident. I could have gone the rest of my life in ignorance.

Derek says good-bye and walks away. I don't stop him even though I don't want to be alone. He shouldn't want to be with me right now, anyway. Not now that he knows. Derek and Dex whisper on the other side of the room, and my stomach jerks. They're talking about *me*. About the monster who helped give me life.

My throat convulses, and I jump to my feet, scrambling for the bathroom. I throw the seat up just in time. My insides spasm and everything I've eaten today comes back up.

Derek is suddenly there, holding my hair. He pats my back, but I just want him to leave me alone. I don't like him seeing me like this, but even worse, I hate him knowing who I really am. How will he be able to stand touching me after learning this? How can he let these hands touch him? I'm the product of a monster.

When the heaving has finally stopped, I shove his hands away and sink to the floor. The bathroom is small and dirty. It smells like vomit and piss, but I can't move. Every inch of my body hurts, and my throat feels like it's closing.

Derek kneels next to me. "Kara."

He turns my face up, but I close my eyes. I'm too ashamed. I'm a monster. That's where I came from, that's what I've spent the last week searching for.

"Kara, please look at me." His voice is desperate, and I can't help but open my eyes. "Talk to me."

"You know. What do you want me to say? That my mom was right? That I wish we'd never started looking? That I wish I'd never been in that accident, so I didn't have to know the truth?"

He flinches and leans back on his heels. "If you hadn't been in that accident you wouldn't have walked into that pool hall. You wouldn't have met me. Doesn't that count for something?"

My throat tightens even more. How am I still able to breathe? His eyes swim with pain. I want to be able to tell him it does count for something, that it somehow makes things better. But I can't. I'm not sure if it's true.

"You're hurting," he says. "I'm sorry, but I can't say that I'm sorry all this happened. I needed you, Kara. I needed you so I could snap out of it. I've been living in limbo for too long."

We stare at each other in silence. What do I say? I won't lie, and I don't know if I can ever be happy about this.

"I want to go home," I finally say.

"Stop it." Derek grips the steering wheel tightly. Like it's someone's neck, and he's trying to strangle the life out of them. "Stop reading it. You're only making it worse."

But I can't. We've been in the car for over an hour, and I can't stop reading. My father is worse than a monster. He's an abomination. *Ten* women. The Internet is overflowing with information. Details about the victims and how he killed them, even crime scene photos. My head spins, but I can't look away. Every page gives me more insight into this man, but none of it is comforting. How could my mom have dated him? How could *this* be my father?

"Kara." Derek's voice is thick with pain, but I haven't spoken to him since we left. I can't make myself talk, especially not about this. No one will ever understand.

The ride home goes by in a blink of an eye. Derek pulls into my driveway, and I have the door open before he even puts the car in park. I stumble up the walkway. It's icy and I slip a few times, but I manage not to fall. Derek isn't there to steady me.

The door opens before I have a chance to knock, and my mom's face is pale when she steps out onto the icy porch.

"Why?" I scream. "You should have told me! You shouldn't have let me find out around strangers!"

Every inch of my body throbs. My chest aches and my stomach feels weighed down, like I've swallowed a bunch of rocks. My head pounds. Tears roll down my cheeks, and my legs wobble. I have to lean against the side of the house to keep from falling.

"Kara."

She's crying. Reaching for me, but I push her aside and stumble into the house. It's foreign to me now. The comfort I've always known at coming home is gone, and now it feels like a tomb—hollow and silent. I spin around, trying to figure out what it was about this building that used to make me feel so at ease. I come up empty.

"Kara, you have to let me explain."

She follows me into the living room, and I drop onto the couch. "Talk," I whisper. "Tell me how you could let it all turn into this." All the rage has melted away, and I can't even come up with enough energy to raise my head.

"I loved him."

I flinch. How can that be what it all comes down to? "How could you love him? He was a monster."

She kneels in front of me and tries to take my hands, but I jerk away. "Kara, just listen. He wasn't like that with me. With me he was charming and loving, and he worshipped me. He was my professor for years, but I never thought anything would happen. I was happy with your father—"

I move away from her, trying to sink further into the couch. "*He* was my father."

My mom shakes her head. "No. Greg Jones is your father. He always has been."

I clench my fists, digging my nails into my palms. "Tell me the truth. All of it."

Mom stands up. She moves to the other side of the room and sits in the chair furthest from me. "I was going to grad school and dating Greg, and I was happy. But I started spending a lot of time with Professor Stark. He singled me out for attention." She pauses and looks down at her hands. "I didn't intend for anything to happen, but one night he kissed me, and I let him. That was all at first. I felt bad for cheating, and I made up my mind never to let it happen again, but I couldn't stop thinking about him. Eventually, we started having an affair."

"Amy said there was some overlap, between da—Greg and Professor Stark."

"Amy. That's how you found out." She runs her hand

through her hair. It's messy and greasy. "It was just a few weeks. I knew I needed to choose between the two of them. I was in love with JJ—that was his nickname."

"I know."

She bites down on her lower lip like she's trying to draw blood. "I found out I was pregnant a week after I broke up with Greg, and Amy was the only person I told. I was waiting for the right time to tell JJ, but before I had a chance he was arrested."

She stands up and walks to the window. "I thought it wasn't true." Her voice is lower now, barely a whisper. "I thought they'd release him and say it had all been a mistake. But when they searched the house—" Her hand goes to her mouth, and she closes her eyes, but she doesn't need to tell me. I read all about it on the Internet.

"They found the evidence."

She presses her hand against her mouth, like she's trying to smother herself. Or keep the truth from coming out. "I almost died. For a week I didn't eat or sleep. Amy was by my side the entire time. Everyone else thought I had the flu—but she knew better. She wanted me to have an abortion, but I couldn't."

"Because you were raised Catholic." I'd already connected the dots on the drive home. My grandmother was a devote Catholic, and even though Mom doesn't go to church, there are things she still clings to. "So Greg turned out to be your only option." My voice is hard and the words leave a bitter taste in my mouth.

She doesn't even deny it. "I told him the baby was his, and he offered to marry me."

"But you knew?"

She drops her hand and finally turns back to face me. Her eyes shimmer like glass; they look so pale in this light. Almost colorless. "Not for sure. It was possible—"

"When did you realize? When did you know for sure?"

"After you were born. You have your father's mouth."

I press my fist against my gut, trying to ease the

churning in my stomach. "Didn't you think we'd find out? You should have told us."

"I hoped you never would. Look at you. Wasn't it better not knowing? I tried to warn you. Trust me, I know. I've had to live with this every day of my life. The knowledge that I loved that man, and let him touch me— that he and I created a life." She shakes her head and looks at the ground. Tears fall to her feet.

"Did he know about me?"

"No. I never told him. He still has no idea."

My head jerks up. "Still?"

Her eyes hold mine, and I can't move. It's like I'm frozen. "He's still alive."

I can't breathe. I get to my feet, clutching at air. Trying to find something to hold onto. "What do you mean? I read that he was sentenced to death."

She takes a tiny step toward me, but I back away. "He's still on death row," she says quietly. "The sentence hasn't been carried out yet."

I gasp and stumble. She tries to grab me, but I push her away. "Don't touch me," I hiss. My shin hits the coffee table, and I stagger, almost falling. I grip the curtains to keep myself up.

"Kara, please!"

I keep moving, out of the living room and down the hall. It takes forever to get to the front door, and my mom yells after me every step of the way. But I rip the door open and stumble outside without looking back.

The cold air smacks into me, and I run forward, but my foot lands on a patch of ice. I slide across the driveway and hit a snowdrift that has hardened and turned into an icy hill. My face slams into the snow when I fall, and it's like being punched by Frosty the Snowman. Stars burst in my already fuzzy vision.

Footsteps crunch toward me, and I roll over. My entire body is covered in snow, and I shiver, but I can't move. I just lay on my back, letting the ice soak through my clothes, and stare up at the blue sky.

"Kara."

Derek.

He kneels down next to me. "Are you okay?"

"I'll never be okay again." Look at that, I can talk.

He touches my knee, and I wince. "You're bleeding."

Am I? Funny, I didn't even realize I'd gotten hurt. I had no idea it was possible to be numb and in pain at the same time.

"Kara?"

I blink and manage to turn my head. Derek frowns.

"Come on." He scoops me up. I put my arms around his neck, and he carries me to his car. It's still running.

"Did you wait for me?"

He kisses the top of my head, and I close my eyes. "I waited."

I'm still shivering when Derek gets me back to his place. He practically drags me inside, not even bothering to take my shoes off. They leave a trail of dirty footprints across the carpet. I'll have to clean that for him.

He leads me to the couch and shoves me down before going into the other room. At least it feels like a shove. I'm not sure because none of this seems real. My knee throbs, but I don't move.

"Take off your pants," Derek says when he comes back. He puts a bottle of hydrogen peroxide on the table and kneels in front of me. "I need to clean that cut."

"It isn't that bad."

"Doesn't matter, I want to do it anyway."

I get to my feet—my legs are wobbly—and pull down my jeans. If this hadn't been the most horrible day of my life, I would make a crack about him just wanting to get in my pants.

He dabs a cotton ball on my knee, and I wince when it

burns. "Sorry."

I don't take my eyes off the cut. It's a jagged one-inch red mark that slices across my kneecap. "It isn't the most painful thing I've been through today. Someone could shoot me, and it wouldn't even come close."

"So things didn't go well with your mom?"

"You could say that."

Derek blows on my knee, and I shiver, and then he gently covers it with a Band-Aid. When he looks up, his brown eyes are more comforting than a warm bath. "Are you cold?"

"I'm not sure. Everything feels…muddled."

Derek brushes my hair back, and I close my eyes. I lean into his hand and my heart aches. Being with him here is so amazing. It's how I used to feel in my parent's house. Will it ever feel like home to me again?

"I'm sorry," I whisper. "I wouldn't trade me and you, not for anything."

"Open your eyes." His lips brush against my forehead and move down to my nose. "Something happened before you made that phone call. Something we never got to talk about."

"We had sex."

The corner of his mouth turns up. "Not that. I told you I loved you."

That's right. How could I have forgotten? "I said it back."

Derek nods slowly, and his brown eyes flicker back and forth, searching mine. "Did you mean it?"

Until that moment I hadn't thought about Derek in terms of love—only that I felt better around him than anyone else. But the words came out so naturally. It wasn't something I had to think about, and I don't have to now either. Just looking at Derek makes my chest tighten in a way that isn't at all uncomfortable. In fact, it's the most amazing thing I've ever felt.

I swallow. "I did."

His mouth curls into a smile and he touches my cheek. His thumb caresses the corner of my mouth for just as second, and my skin tingles. "No matter what else happens, remember that I love you, and I will be here for you."

CHAPTER NINETEEN

"I can't believe he's still alive."

I tap a fingernail against the laptop and stare at the screen where Jonathon Jacob Stark smiles back at me. He's about my age in the picture. His hair is dark like mine, and slightly wavy. It looks thick. His eyes are soft brown, almost the color of caramel, and his smile is friendly. He's attractive. The kind of guy who would get voted homecoming king or cause a cat fight in the cafeteria at school.

Does he look like me? My eyes sweep over his face, taking in every one of his features. It's hard to tell.

"Do I look like him?"

Derek presses his lips together and shrugs, but he doesn't say anything.

"You can say it." I don't want him to.

"You have his smile."

My stomach twists and I close the window. I can't look at his face anymore. "Why hasn't his sentence been carried out yet?"

Derek rubs my back. He's pretty much been doing that nonstop since we started searching the Internet. "It does seem like a long time, but they have a whole appeal process to go through before they can put a person to death."

"Nineteen years, though? I had no idea a person could sit on death row for so long. How does something like that happen?"

Derek points at the screen. "His execution has been delayed a few times while they dealt with his appeals."

Appeals? The whole thing seems ridiculous! I inhale and push the computer off my lap. "But he's admitted to doing all this. How can an appeal matter at all? He's guilty."

"It looks like they're trying to get his sentence commuted to life in prison. Sometimes appeals don't have anything to do with innocence. Sometimes it's more about finding loopholes or mistakes the prosecution made during trial." Derek sounds like an expert.

"Watch a little too much *Law and Order*?" I jump to my feet. "That's just wrong."

My chest is tight again. I pace the room and try to focus on breathing. The more I search the Internet, the more my insides hurt. It's like I'm being crushed from the inside out.

"If it makes you feel better, he's scheduled to be executed in April."

I stop walking. My hand flies to my mouth, and there's strange twist in the bottom of my stomach I don't understand. Why? I've never had mixed feelings about the death penalty—an eye for an eye. This man is a monster. He deserves to die, and the families of his victims deserve to know justice has been served. Nineteen years is long enough.

But I'm curious about him. I can't help it. What was it about this man that made my mom love him? How could he have loved one woman while killing others? There's virtually no information about his childhood online. All it says is his parents are dead, and he had a younger brother. Nothing else. No one really knows who he is. And even if they did, there are things about him books and the Internet won't be able to tell me. Only he can.

The thought catches me off guard and my stomach rolls. Clutching my belly, I bend over and suck in a deep breath. There's nothing in it to throw up, but it still convulses. Derek rubs my back, but it doesn't help. Nothing ever will. The pain rolling through me is here for the rest of my life, threatening to eat me alive.

"Are you alright?"

"Is it crazy to want to meet him?" My voice is barely a whisper. It's like I'm afraid to say it too loud.

Derek's hand stops moving. "What?"

Slowly, I turn to face him. "I want to understand."

Derek's hand drops to his side. His lips move a few times before he finally says, "Why he killed women? I don't think meeting him will help with that. He's crazy, Kara. The psychiatrists that have examined him said so."

Massaging my scalp, I shake my head and stare at the floor. I don't want to meet Derek's eyes. "Not that. I don't want to know about that. I want to know how this man could have made my mom love him. How she could have broken up with my da—Greg Jones for this monster? Did he love her back?"

"You can't meet him, Kara."

I look up. "Why not?"

"Because he's crazy. Because it's dangerous."

"He's behind bars, Derek. He can't hurt me."

"Maybe not physically, but mentally or emotionally he could destroy you. He's a sociopath."

There's a little part of me that acknowledges how right Derek is. But what if I don't go see him, and I regret it the rest of my life? Maybe his execution will be rescheduled again, but eventually he will be put to death. Then I'll have lost my only opportunity to meet him.

"There has to be another way. Family or something." Derek runs his hand through his hair. "Or your mom! You should sit down and talk with your mom, Kara. That makes more sense than going to see him."

"You're right."

But even my mom can't tell me everything. There may be something Stark can tell me even she doesn't know, something seeing him with my own eyes will explain.

Derek studies me like he can read my thoughts. "Why don't you get together with your dad?"

My whole body jerks. He means my *dad*, not Jonathon Stark. "Yeah. That's something I need to do."

Derek slides a beer across the counter, but my stomach is doing somersaults. No way will I be able to keep it down. Gray Beard wasn't thrilled to see me, but he gave Derek his job back. Just like Derek said he would.

"What's his deal, anyway?" I ask, jerking my head toward Gray Beard. The pirate scowls at me, and I have the urge to salute him.

"Old family friend." Derek glances over his shoulder toward Gray Beard. "He's just trying to look out for me."

That explains why he lets Derek come and go like this. "So does he search for booty in his spare time?"

Derek grins. "Not the kind you're talking about." I laugh, but it doesn't feel real. "He's not a fan of the pirate jokes."

"I kind of figured."

The bell rings. I turn just as the door shuts behind my dad. My insides tighten, and I grip my glass. His eyes meet mine. They're dark, and his shoulders are slumped. His clothes are wrinkled. I've never seen him like this. What has he been going through? My vision blurs and without thinking I take a sip of my beer.

My dad doesn't smile when he stops in front of me. "Hey baby."

Everything inside me crumbles, and I fall against him, crying. "Daddy."

His body stiffens, then relaxes. Then his arms are

around me and it's just like when I was little. He rubs my head and my entire body shakes.

"It's okay. I'm sorry, Kara. I've been so selfish." He pulls away and looks down at me. His eyes shimmer. "You must have been going through hell."

He has no idea. I lay my head against his chest. All day, I've been trying to decide what to tell him. He deserves to know what really happened, but now that he's here I can't help wondering how he'll handle it. Will the truth be too much for him? Is it too much for me? Right now, it feels like it.

He pulls back, and I tilt my face up toward his. "I don't think I can forgive your mom," he says. "What she did was awful. But you will always be my daughter, Kara. Don't think that's changed."

He kisses my forehead, and I try to embrace his words. Try to erase the truth. *This* is my dad. Not Jonathon Stark. Greg Jones is the man who raised me, who sat with me when I was sick, who helped me with homework and took me to the hospital when I broke my arm. That other man is not a part of me.

But the tears escape just like the truth—Jonathon Stark gave me life. Nothing I do will ever take that away.

And my dad deserves to know what really happened. The lies have to stop.

I step back and wipe the tears off my cheeks. "We need to talk."

Dad sniffs, but he still doesn't cry. My hands shake when I lead him toward the most secluded table, and my palms are moist. I wipe them on my pants. Thankfully, it's still early and there are only two other patrons in the bar. We don't need a big audience.

Dad sits across from me. He frowns, and the lines on his face look deeper than ever. He's aged years in the past few weeks. "What is it?"

My throat is tight. I should just say it, but I can't seem to get any words out. "My real father."

His face scrunches up. "She told you who it was?"

I clear my throat and dig my nails into my palms. "She wouldn't."

He nods and looks down. Does he know? Did she confess to him before I found out? I can't tell what he's thinking.

"She wouldn't tell me either."

Of course not. "I found out on my own."

He slowly raises his head. His gray eyes swim with pain. "I'm not sure if I want to know, Kara."

I laugh, I can't help it. "I understand. There's a part of me that wishes I'd never looked. But I think it might help you understand."

His eyes get bigger. "Why? What's wrong?"

My mouth goes dry. I swallow, but it doesn't help, and I wish I had something to drink. My beer is still sitting on the bar. "My real father is Dr. Jonathon Stark."

Dad sits back. He blinks a few times, and his mouth hangs open. Then his hands fall to his sides, and he doesn't move.

We stare at each other, and I start to count. I make it to fifty-nine before he finally speaks.

"No wonder she lied." He runs his hand down his face. "She should have told me." He doesn't look at me.

So Amy Ceccoli was right. He would have taken her back, anyway. I'm not surprised really. He's a good man. The exact opposite of my real father. How could my mom have chosen two men so different from one another?

He stares at his hands, and a hundred emotions cross his face. Pain, frustration…understanding. He looks at me, and his eyes are softer. "Now I get it."

What does he get? Why she lied to him, or why she lied to me? "Would you have told me if you'd known?"

He opens his mouth, and then slams it shut. He leans back. He rubs his chin for a few seconds. "I don't know."

My eyes burn and I shake my head, trying to keep the tears buried inside. "So you would have lied too?" Of course. Honesty is something parents have to teach their children, but it doesn't obligate them to tell the truth. Do as I say, not as I do.

"Kara, what your mom did…" He shakes his head. "She should have told me the truth. She misled me for nineteen years."

I slam my hand on the table. "She did the same thing to me!"

He takes my hand, and I want to pull it away. His touch stings. Or maybe it's his words. "She did it to protect you. I'm not sure if I would have done things differently."

I pull my hand out of his and put it in my lap. Even if Mom had been honest with him in the very beginning, I would have ended up in this exact position. Hurt and betrayed, confused. Only it would have been worse—a double betrayal.

"Kara, you just said you wished you'd never looked. Maybe your mom wasn't completely wrong?"

"I don't know. There's a part of me that wishes I could go back. But maybe if she'd been honest from the very beginning it would have made things easier. Would have softened the blow."

"Try to understand where your mother is coming from."

"So now you're defending her? Just a few minutes ago you told me you'd never be able to forgive her!"

My voice echoes through the bar and the few people that are here turn to look at us. Behind the counter, Derek tilts his head to the side and mouths, *do you need me?* Yes. I *do* need him. More than I need air. But that's not what he means, so I shake my head.

"I didn't understand. I just thought she'd cheated on me, Kara. But this!" He pinches the bridge of his nose. "I guess there are gray areas in life."

"No, there aren't. I understand not telling me when I was five—but the way I found out is unforgivable." Even as I say it, I know it isn't true, but I'm not ready to give up my anger yet. I need time.

"Apparently, there isn't much that's unforgivable when it comes to the people you love."

It sure didn't take long for him to change his tune. Not that I'm surprised; he's too understanding. I could learn a lot from him.

"So you're just going to stay mad at her forever?"

As usual, he seems to be reading my mind. We've always been on the same page. Been allies. It all seems so ironic now.

There's no way I can meet his gaze right now. I don't want to see the disappointment in his eyes, so I focus on the little half-moons in my palms from where I dug my nails in. They're red. I almost broke the skin.

"Kara." He's using *that* tone. The one I've heard a million times over the years. It's his dad voice.

"I don't know."

"Let's talk about something else."

When I look up, his face is so much softer than just a few minutes ago. He's a saint. He went from hating her to deciding to forgive her in less than ten minutes. She'll never know how lucky she is.

Then again, all she has to do is think about Stark.

Dad gets up and holds his hand out to me. "First, let's get a drink."

"I'm not twenty-one."

"I saw the beer when I walked in." I start to argue, but he raises his hand to stop me. "I'm not going to ground you. It's not like I didn't do some underage drinking myself." He smiles. It's still a little strained, but it looks more like him. "Fake ID?"

I clear my throat and tilt my head toward the bar. Toward Derek. "I started seeing someone. He works here." Dad glances that way and frowns. Despite how dead I feel inside, I find myself smiling. "He's a good guy. He's been there for me."

Dad nods and puts his arm around my shoulder. "Then

I'm sure I'll love him. Someone should have been there for you." He kisses the top of my head and leads me toward the bar. "I'm sorry it wasn't me."

CHAPTER TWENTY

My eyes are starting to hurt, but I still don't feel the least bit tired. I glance at the display on the bottom of the screen. It's almost four o'clock in the morning. No wonder my eyes are burning. I've been on the computer for over four hours.

I rub my eyes, and then lean back and stretch until the muscles in my shoulders pop. Everything hurts from being hunched over, but I've managed to learn a lot. And all of it comes down to one simple fact: I don't have much time to find out who I really am.

Jonathon Stark is scheduled to be executed on April tenth. That gives me less than three months. If I want to visit him, reservations have to be made thirty days in advance. Around thirty days before his execution he'll have a clemency hearing, but there's no way he'll be granted clemency. Not only is the governor very pro-capital punishment, but he was actually living in Kent at the time of the murder. He even knew one of the victims. There's no doubt in my mind Jonathon Stark will be put to death on April tenth.

I've already printed out the visitor packet and e-mailed the Chillicothe Correctional Institution to request a reservation for February twelfth. Derek is just going to love that. Not that I'm doing somersaults or anything, but my stomach is. I'm still not sure it's what I want to do. The thought of going to see him terrifies me, but so does the thought of him dying and me losing the chance. I can always cancel the reservations if I change my mind.

There's loads of information online about Stark's trial and arrest, the murders—most I couldn't stomach reading—and his time at the university. But I'm still having trouble finding anything but generic information about his youth. Most of his early life is still a mystery. His dad was in the Air Force, and they moved around a lot, but he never had any trouble with the law and everyone they've interviewed that does remember him says he was nice. Well-liked, even. It's disturbing. How much of a psycho is this guy who managed to fool everyone until he was well into his thirties?

Maybe there will be some answers in the books that have been written about him—there are gobs of those. Books about serial killers with chapters dedicated to Stark, case studies of his crimes and even a few biographies. There's one in particular I want to pick up. It's called *Stark Contrast*, and it's written by a psychiatrist who interviewed him on several occasions. The only regular interviews he's ever given.

I need to go to a bookstore today.

My eyes are closed when footsteps pad into the room behind me. Derek brushes the hair off my shoulder and presses his lips to my neck. "What are you doing up?"

He continues kissing my shoulder, then moves my shirt aside so his lips can travel down my chest. I keep my eyes closed and exhale slowly through my nose. "I couldn't sleep." His lips work magic on me.

"Come back to bed," he whispers against my skin.

"I won't be able to sleep."

"Who said anything about sleep?"

He spins the chair around, and his lips move up to mine. Then his hands slide up my legs to my thighs, and he pulls back, grinning. "You're not wearing any underwear."

I run my fingers through his hair and kiss the tip of his nose. "I like sleeping naked."

"I like it when you sleep naked."

He stands up, pulling me with him, but he doesn't move. My hands slide out of his. Derek is staring at the desk, and my heart skips about four beats. Crap.

He picks up the visitation packet. "What's this?"

I swallow. "You have to fill these out before you can visit someone."

His face scrunches up and he shakes his head, but he doesn't look at me. "Kara, no. *No.*"

"I don't want to fight about this."

He tosses the forms aside and runs his hand through his hair. It immediately falls back over his eyebrow. I try to brush it aside, but he flinches like my hand is a snake or a deadly weapon.

"Don't do this."

"Why? What's the big deal?" I'm having a really hard time understanding why he's so upset about this.

"It's dangerous. I already told you that."

"He's going to be behind glass. What are you afraid is going to happen?"

When he looks up his brown eyes are huge. "What am I afraid of? Losing you! What else?"

When I move toward him, he steps back and bumps into the wall. I take another step until there's only a few inches of space between us. He won't meet my eyes. "Derek, nothing is going to happen. He's locked up, he's about to be put to death."

"You don't know that."

"Derek, look at me."

He slowly raises his head.

"Nothing is going to happen. Okay?"

He shoves off the wall, practically pushing me aside. "I'm going back to bed."

So much for sex. I guess talking about visiting my serial

killer dad is a mood killer.

I'm massaging my head when Derek puts the coffee in front of me, my second one since we got to the bookstore. "My head is going to explode."

He plops into the chair opposite me coffeeless. One cup usually does it for him. "Still nothing?"

I inhale slowly and shake my head. "Nope." I pop the P like a bubble. "This man is a mystery. He's in his fifties now, but somehow managed to go through his entire life without actually allowing anyone to really get to know him."

"His family is all dead but the brother?"

I shut the book in front of me and shove it aside. "Yup, and no one knows where he is. He changed his name after the arrest and has disappeared. Can't say I blame him."

I look up when Derek starts tapping his pen against the table. His face is all scrunched up like whatever he's thinking hurts. The table is littered with books and paper and empty coffee cups, but I still have a whole list of unanswered questions.

"You need to talk to your mom."

I groan. "I know. But there's no guarantee she'll even tell me anything."

My leg starts to shake. I cross my ankles and work on keeping still. "This lady seems to have the most information about Stark." I tap the book in front of me. "Anne Rohr is the psychiatrist that was working for the state when he was arrested. He trusted her."

I flip the book over and stare at the woman's smiling face. She's pretty. Wavy brown hair and light blue eyes. No wonder Stark confided in her. "She can probably tell me something."

"Then you wouldn't have to meet with him." Derek

sounds hopeful.

"There are things that no one will be able to tell me but him, Derek." I refuse to give him false hope; I know I won't cancel that meeting. As much as it makes me want to hurl to think about sitting face-to-face with Stark, I can't just walk away from this.

He presses his lips together. "We need to find the brother. He could answer questions."

"He's gone. Vanished. Don't you think someone would have found him if they could?"

"We could hire a private investigator."

When I reach for my coffee, my hand is shaking. I need to lay off the caffeine. "I can't even imagine how much money that would cost. It's not like I can ask my parents to pay for it or anything, and I don't have a job."

"I can pay for it."

"I'm not taking your money. That's for you live on."

"I have plenty. The house and cars are all paid for—it's not like I have anything else to spend it on."

"It won't last forever, and it's not like you're making any other money or anything. I'm sure your graphic novel is wonderful, but there's no guarantee it will get published." I shuffle the papers in front of me into a neat pile and take a deep breath, trying to keep it casual. "You don't really seem to have much of a plan for the future."

Even though I can tell he's trying to maintain his relaxed attitude, his jaw twitches. "Don't see much of a point."

"Why?"

"One day at a time. That's what I have to focus on." He taps the pen faster, and I put my hand on his. He still doesn't meet my eyes.

Until now, I'd really thought he was doing a good job of dealing with his family. He isn't. He's drifting, ignoring reality.

"You can't spend the rest of your life like this."

"Like what? I'm just trying to enjoy the time I have. It

seems stupid to waste time working or going to school when I don't have to."

"Derek…" I scoot my chair closer and lower my voice. "Just because your family died doesn't mean that your time here is limited. You could live to be a hundred."

He finally looks at me. "That isn't why. I just don't want to have regrets. I want to live every day like it could be my last."

"You think just because you get an education you can't have fun? You can still live a full life and do all the things you planned to do before."

"I'm trying, Kara. I told you before how good you are for me, and I meant it. Doing all this may seem easy for me, but some mornings just getting out of bed is an effort. With you here it's been easier. You've given me a reason to get up, to eat, to get dressed. To care about something." His eyes shimmer. He clears his throat and swipes his hand through his hair.

"I'm glad I'm helping you, but I still think you could do more. You're too smart to be working in that hole and drifting through life like you don't have anything to offer the world. Trust me—the world is a better place because you're here."

His lips turn up into a shaky smile. "So you keep saying."

Then he lets out a big sigh. Slowly, his jaw and shoulders start to relax. "Okay. Since I haven't made any New Year's resolutions, except to have lots of sex with you, and well—" he elbows me "—mission accomplished." He grins and my cheeks actually get warm. "I'll look into school for the fall."

He kisses my neck. Warmth spreads through my stomach and my cheeks get hotter. My legs start to shake again. I press my heels into the floor to keep them from tapping. How can just a little kiss on the neck send me over the edge?

"Which brings up something I've been meaning to talk

to you about."

"What's that?" I exhale and try to ignore the warmth spreading through my body.

"School." His lips are pursed. "Are you planning on going back?"

Oh. Crap. I've been so busy lately that I haven't thought any further ahead than the next few weeks. The fall semester seems light-years away right now. "I don't know."

He gently strokes the top of my hand. "I don't want you to go. You could transfer."

To Wright State? It seems like such a step down. It's not like Ohio University is Harvard or anything (or MIT!), but Wright State is such a commuter school. It's where people who aren't serious about college go.

But will he feel abandoned if I leave?

"I'll think about it." We have months to deal with all this. There's no point in upsetting him now.

I hold the book in front of Derek's face and tap Anne Rohr's picture. "I need to get in touch with her."

He nods and pulls out his laptop; I'm glad he brought it now. "Okay. Well, let's start with the Internet. Maybe she has a website?"

It's worth a shot. We Google Anne Rohr and get about a million hits—most of which have to do with Stark. Apparently, she's made quite a name for herself since his arrest. Derek finds her official web site and clicks on the link. When it opens a picture of Stark flash across the screen, followed by faces of other men I don't recognize. Other serial killers maybe? The slide show plays itself out after a few seconds. When it's finally over and the website comes up, I manage to relax.

Derek clicks on Anne Rohr's picture, and her biographical information pops up. "So she was the original psychiatrist that examined him after he was arrested," he says. "But now it looks like she's considered one of the top experts on antisocial personality disorder."

"Isn't that what Stark was diagnosed with?"

He scrolls down. "Yup. And since then she's interviewed him and other serial killers hundreds of times, written four books and dozens of papers. She's been busy." He points at the screen. "Look at her lecture schedule."

"Great. So basically we're going to have a hell of a time getting in touch with her."

"I don't know. There's a phone number right here, and it says you can contact her about speaking engagements. You could call it and leave a message."

"It's not like I have any other options." I pull out my phone. "The area code is six one four—Columbus?"

"Her PO box is a Columbus address."

"No way she still lives in Ohio!" We can't be that lucky. Everything else so far has been like a game of connect the dots. If Rohr lives an hour away I'm probably going to have a stroke.

I dial the number and hold my breath. After thirty seconds the voicemail picks up. "You have reached the voicemail of Dr. Anne Rohr. If you are interested in booking me for a speaking engagement, please leave your name, number, the date and the company or institution you are affiliated with."

It beeps and I take a deep breath. "Dr. Rohr, my name is Kara Jones, and my mother was a student of Jonathon Stark's at Kent State. This may sound insane, but I recently discovered that they were having an affair while she was there and—" I glance at Derek "—that Jonathon Stark is my biological father. Since you seem to be an expert on him, I was hoping you'd be willing to speak with me." I leave my phone number, press end, and exhale slowly through my nose.

"Now we just have to wait," Derek says.

And hope she doesn't think I'm crazy.

CHAPTER TWENTY-ONE

"I want you to come with me," I say.

My legs start to shakes the second Derek pulls into the driveway. Dad's car is here. Will him being here make this whole thing better or worse? I'm not sure.

Derek pats my leg, but I don't make a move to open the door even when he pulls the key out of the ignition. My body feels like it's fused to the seat.

"We don't have to do this today, Kara." Derek keeps patting my leg.

He's wrong. We do have to do this today. I need to know the whole story or my head will explode. Plus, I have to know what my mom knows about Stark before I meet with this biographer. When she gets back to me.

I finally manage to get my arms to work. "It's okay," I say, opening the door. "I have to deal with it sooner or later. Putting it off isn't going to make it any easier."

The front door opens before we've reached the porch, and my dad steps out. He smiles and gives me a big hug, but I can't force my body to relax. All the stress of the other night is gone, and the worry lines have disappeared from his face. The life is back in his eyes. He's like a new man. How can he have adjusted so fast?

Dad kisses the top of my head before patting Derek on

the shoulder. "I was just talking about the two of you. Your mom was worried, but I told her what a help Derek has been."

He tries to pull me into the house, but my feet are glued to the porch. I can't wrap my mind around this whole thing. Between my mom and Stark, my mom and Dad, me and my mom—there's just too much going on. My head aches, and I massage my temples. I can't look away from him.

"So that's it?" I ask. "You're able to forget everything that fast?"

"I'm going to work on it," he says.

I grimace, and he shakes his head.

"Kara, I'm not sure if you'll ever be able to understand why I've made this decision." His eyes move to Derek, and his lips tighten. "Or maybe one day you will. I love your mom, which is why I thought I couldn't forgive her. The idea of her being with someone else just hurt too much. Now that I know the whole story—well, I can't really say I blame her."

I blink, and it takes me a few seconds to fully process his words. They bounce around in my brain like a ball in a pinball machine, only dropping into the slot after doing a lot of damage. "But she still cheated on you." I want to stick up for my dad, even if he won't stick up for himself. What she did was wrong.

"You can't know what he was like. The power he had over people…" He clenches his jaw and something flashes in his eyes, but he blinks, and it's gone before I can figure out what it was. "Well, let's just leave it at that."

My throat constricts even more; it's like there's a noose tightening around my neck. He knew Stark too? "You've met him?" My voice comes out scratchy.

Dad's eyes cloud over and fill with…anger? Fear? It's hard to say. "Yes." He barely opens his mouth, and the word has to squeeze its way between his teeth.

I wait for him to say more, but he doesn't, and I shiver

when the wind blows. Derek lets go of my hand and puts his arm around my shoulders. But by the time Dad drags me into the house my entire body is shivering. Only it isn't from the frigid temperatures.

Mom stands in the living room. Her eyes gleam, and she looks back and forth between me and Dad like she's afraid we're going to disappear. Dad starts to cross the room to her, but stops halfway. He looks back at me and tilts his head to the side, but I stay in the doorway. No one says a word. Derek slides his hand back into mine, and I dig my nails into it, trying to find a way to make my mouth move. Mom just keeps staring at me, and her body jerks a little like she's ready to run to my side. But I cringe away from her, and she stops.

"I'm making a roast," she finally says. "When your dad said he was coming over I just knew I had to make his favorite." Just like dad, she looks more put together. Her hair and makeup are done; her clothes are clean. She still has dark circles under her eyes, but she looks better than she has since the day of my accident.

"A roast sounds good," Derek says at the exact moment I say, "We're not staying."

Dad pats my back. "Of course you are. It will give your mother and me a chance to get to know Derek a little. The two of you have been spending quite a bit of time together." He frowns and shakes his head a little. I guess Mom told him I've been sleeping at Derek's.

Dad clears his throat and motions toward the couch. "Derek, why don't you and I sit in here while the ladies work on dinner?"

It would be an insanely sexist statement if it actually had anything to do with dinner, but it doesn't. My dad gives me a smile stretched so tight it looks more like a grimace and nods his head toward my mom. Yeah, I get it Dad. Play nice. I'm not sure if I can, though.

My mom's smile is shaky, and doesn't look the least bit sincere as she heads for the kitchen. I'm torn. There's a part of me that would rather have my nails ripped out than talk to her, but another part of me *needs* to have this moment. My curiosity over Stark is too strong to walk away from, so I follow her into the kitchen.

She's shaking in her socks when she stops in the middle of the room and grips the island like she's floating in the ocean, and it's her only salvation. I get it, though. We all need something to hold onto. My strong family has always been my island. What do I have now? Lies and skeletons, and a father who tortured women for fun. The thought makes my stomach jump to my throat, and I almost choke on it.

But I swallow and meet my mom's blue eyes. "I want you to tell me everything."

She grimaces. The skin at the corners of her eyes crinkles and three lines appear on her forehead. This is what I will look like in twenty years—if I'm lucky. As pissed as I am, I can't deny how well she's aged or how lucky I am to look like her. Thank God I don't have her personality.

Does that mean I have *his?* The thought makes my skin crawl.

Mom loosens her grip on the island and turns to the oven. She slowly pulls the door open. "You're sure? Remember Kara, you can't unlearn something."

I'm glad she's not looking at me. She wouldn't like the disgust on my face when I say, "Not true." I lean against the counter. There's an open bottle of wine next to me, and I pour myself a glass. "I *unlearned* trust."

She may have her back to me, but I don't miss it when her shoulders tense. She takes her time checking the temperature of the meat, and I swallow a big gulp of the wine. It's not really my thing, but right now I need alcohol almost as much as I need air.

"I met Jonathon Stark when I started my graduate degree," she says, slowly shutting the door and turning to face me. Her eyes go to the glass of wine in my hand, but she doesn't scold me. Instead, she walks over and pours herself a glass—a much bigger glass than mine—and takes a long drink. When she sets it down she licks her lips. "He was the most charismatic man I had ever met. Even now, I've never met anyone else like him." I flinch, and she shrugs. "You'll never be able to understand, but remember this—I was not the only person who fell under his spell. *Everyone* loved him. His classes were the first to get full. He was invited to parties, and female students threw themselves at him. JJ was like a celebrity at Kent."

"But he chose you." My voice shakes, so I take another sip of wine. Hopefully, it will help numb my emotions as well as my senses.

Mom nods and taps a finger against her glass. The burgundy liquid sloshes around, coming dangerously close to jumping over the rim, but she doesn't stop. "He singled me out. Your father and I had been dating for about six months. I cared about him a great deal, but I wasn't sure if I loved him the way he loved me. And JJ was so charming."

I swallow when bile rises in my throat. It was bad enough when my dad said it, but *this*. The wistful tone in her voice, the faraway look in her eyes… I take another drink and focus on staring at the glass, so I don't have to look at her.

"The first few times he suggested I come to his house I turned him down. I told him I was seeing someone, but he was persistent, and it was so flattering. Every girl in the school wanted him." She steps closer, but I don't look up from my glass. "Don't judge me, Kara. Please."

"I'm trying." It isn't working. The judgment rolls through me like a heat wave, making my blood come dangerously close to boiling point. I don't care if every other person at Kent fell under Stark's charms, what I care about is my family.

Mom walks to the other side of the kitchen, and I finally rip my eyes away from my glass. She leans against the counter, and her entire upper body slumps forward like she doesn't have the energy to stand up anymore. Did she know I needed distance from her, or does she need distance from me to finish the story? Either way, I'm glad she's not so close. The constant threat of her trying to touch me is getting to me.

"Then one night he kissed me. We were in his office, and it came out of nowhere. I tried to stop it at first, but he was almost impossible to resist." She swallows. "Afterward, I was determined it wouldn't happen again. JJ was my professor, and it wasn't right. Plus, I was seeing your dad."

She keeps saying that, talking about my dad and JJ like they're two different people. It's hard to convince myself they are, but I need them to be. There's no way I can go through the rest of my life thinking of Stark as my father and not go insane. And Greg Jones is my dad. He *is*.

"But then it happened again, and again, and I knew I needed to make a choice. It was hard, but when it came down to it, I was so much more drawn to JJ…there was something about him, and I couldn't stop thinking about him. He was on my mind constantly."

I can't tear my eyes off her face. She frowns, stares into her wineglass like it will give her the answer to a life-altering question. Her dreamy tone is gone, replaced by some other emotion. Horror or disgust, I'm not sure. She keeps shaking her head and grimacing like she can't believe it all really happened. That makes two of us.

"Why didn't he kill you?" It's all I've been able to think about since I found out. What is it about my mom that saved her? "He was in Kent for a little over two years, and he killed ten women. Why not you?"

"I have no idea. I've thought about that a lot over the last eighteen years. Would he have killed me? Was he leading up to it? I'll never know for sure, but I don't think so. When I broke up with your father, JJ asked me to marry him."

My entire body jerks and my legs wobble. I have to grab the counter so I don't collapse. "What? You were engaged to him?"

Mom nods slowly. Her blue eyes penetrate mine, and she clutches her glass with one hand while curling a chunk of hair around the fingers of her other. Over and over again, swirling then releasing, swirling then releasing. My head spins right along with her hair.

I try to calm down, try to focus. There are too many things I need to know to lose it now. "But the police didn't know? They never questioned you?"

"I never told anyone—except Amy—and obviously JJ didn't either because no one ever came to see me. Our affair was a secret. He would have gotten fired. For some reason, he kept it that way."

I want to vomit. I set the glass down and lean forward, inhaling and exhaling slowly through my nose. "When did you find out about me?"

"Five days before he was arrested. I planned to tell him over dinner that Saturday. I was thrilled, and I just knew he would be too, but the FBI arrested him on Friday. Then my world collapsed." She whispers the last sentence, like she really is buried under a pile of rubble.

I can't look away from her. How much more can I take before my wildly beating heart explodes? There's no way to know for sure, but I do know I can't stop now. I've come too far. "What happened after he was arrested?"

"I didn't believe it." She stops talking. I hold my breath and count, waiting for her to continue. When I get to forty I look up. She's staring at the wall.

"What happened?" My throat and stomach feel like I've swallowed hot coals, and they're baking my insides.

"They searched his house and found skulls in the basement. He had mementos from each of his victims— jewelry and things. There were pictures in his safe." She closes her eyes and leans her head back, breathing slowly. "Then he confessed and I wanted to die."

The coals work their way up to my eyes, and I blink against the burning. My nails are buried in my palms; they're going to draw blood soon. "You never had a clue? There was nothing about him that made you wonder if things weren't quite right?" I just can't believe she was that close to him, and she had no idea. He had to show some sign of violence or anger. *Something.*

But she shakes her head. "No. I told you, he was amazing. He was a gentleman and when we were together he treated me like I was the only woman in the world. On the surface, he was the perfect man."

I'm starting to get a clearer picture of Stark, but there are still so many things I want to know and my mom's description of him only adds more questions to my list. Their relationship doesn't follow any of his normal patterns. With his other victims, he didn't have an actual relationship, and most weren't even in his department, which is why the police had a difficult time linking him to the victims. It almost seems like he really was going to marry my mother. Maybe it was just to keep up appearances? Is it possible he really loved her?

Mom and I both jump when the timer goes off. She turns to get the roast out of the oven, and I use it as my chance to escape. There are still things I want to know, but I just can't face anymore right now. I need time to process what I've learned before I take in anything else.

I'm halfway to the living room when my dad's voice makes me stop in my tracks. "I can't say that I'm a fan of Kara being at your house every night."

There's a shuffling sound like Derek's squirming on the couch. I picture his dark hair falling over his eyebrow, and his super Zoloft powers work their magic on me even from the other room. My body relaxes a tad, and I lean my shoulder against the wall. If only we were back in his house, curled up in his bed. Then I'd be safe and comfortable, and I wouldn't have this intense pain in my stomach.

"She hasn't wanted to come home," Derek says.

I can't help smiling. It sounds like the worst excuse in the world.

Dad clears his throat. "I just hope you aren't taking advantage of her. She's vulnerable right now." It's the same tone he uses when he talks to my dates, but the words are very different. Usually he talks about respecting me and having me home on time. I guess this is a unique situation.

"I can understand your concerns, sir."

Sir? Wow. I guess Derek's manners extend further than just opening doors for me.

"I have every intention of being with your daughter for the rest of my life."

My heart constricts, and I rest my head against the wall. The future isn't something we'd really talked about yet, not with how tense the present has been. But I can see it too. Derek and me together years from now. It just makes sense. How did I manage to get so lucky in the middle of this disaster? It doesn't seem possible.

My dad sighs and there's a very awkward pause that stretches on so long it makes my heart pound. "I understand you've been through a lot too. Maybe this is good for both of you. Maybe you two are the only ones that will ever really be able to understand what the other person has been through."

"She's been good for me." Derek's voice sounds thick, and he clears his throat again. "I think I've been good for her. She says so anyway."

Good for me? Without him, I wouldn't have made it through all this. They would have locked me in a padded room by now.

My phone rings, making me jump, and I bump my head on the wall. "Damn." I rub my head and pull the phone out of my back pocket at the same time. I don't recognize the number, but it's a Columbus area code, and my heart starts to pound harder.

"Hello?" My voice is shaky and doesn't sound the least bit like me.

"Is this Kara Jones?" a female voice asks. She sounds breathless, like she's been running or something.

"Yes."

"Kara, this is Anne Rohr. I got your message and I have to say, I'm intrigued. I'm out of town at the moment, but I'll be back in Ohio the middle of next week. I'd love to get together if we can work it out. I can meet you Thursday if you can come to Columbus, but if I have to come to you, I'm afraid I'll have to wait until the following week. I'm absolutely swamped right now."

Thursday? That's in four days! "I can come to Columbus."

Derek comes into the hall, with my dad right behind him, and raises an eyebrow at me. I shake my head and turn my back to them; I don't want my parents to get wind of what I'm planning. "I can meet you anytime, just shoot me a text and let me know when and where. Okay?"

"Sounds good!" Anne says.

After hanging up, I turn around, but my dad has disappeared.

"Anne?" Derek whispers.

"Next week."

His eyebrows shoot up and disappear under his hair. I brush it aside. He grins, catches my hand in his, and presses it to his lips.

"You and Dad have a nice talk?"

He chuckles. "Oh yeah. He was very interested in me and my plans for the future."

"Dinner!" Mom calls before I can say anything else. Great, just what I wanted.

CHAPTER TWENTY-TWO

My body is covered in a fine sheen of sweat when I lay back against the sheets. I'm panting, and Derek kisses my collar bone. I brush his moist hair off his forehead. "I needed that," I say. "I was too tense after dinner with my parents."

Derek grins, showing off that amazing dimple of his. "It wasn't that bad."

"True, I've been through more uncomfortable things. My first visit to the gynecologist's office comes to mind." I roll onto my side, so I can see him.

Derek's eyes twinkle. "Well, whenever you want to use me to relieve some tension for you…" He wiggles his eyebrows and runs his fingers from my collar bone all the way to my belly button.

I give him a little wink. "Right back at you."

Derek stretches, arching his back and curling his toes. "So what are we doing this week? Hunting for buried treasure? Solving the mysteries of the universe?"

"I plan on resting and having lots of sex."

"Sounds like a good way to spend the week, although I do have to work."

Crap, he's right. Which brings up the very important topic of my future. What the hell am I supposed to do until the fall? It's too late to take spring classes, and a job requires a car.

"Must be nice. I'm a prisoner."

He narrows his eyes and shakes his head. "I don't follow you."

"No car, remember? My mom already said she's not getting me one, and I don't have a job. I think I have a little over a grand in the bank." I flop onto my back. "I guess I could use it as a down payment, but I need a job to apply for a loan, and I can't get a job if I don't have a car to get there."

"I have cars."

I roll back onto my side, so I'm facing him. "Cars? As in, more than one?"

"Mine and my dad's. I've never gotten rid of it." He starts playing with my hair twisting it between his fingers. "It's just sitting in the garage. You can use it."

"Derek—"

He drops my hair and puts his hand over my mouth. "Don't tell me you can't because it doesn't make any difference to me. It's just sitting there, Kara. You may as well use it."

I pull myself forward until our faces are only inches apart. "Do you have any idea how amazing you are? I doubt I'll ever be able to pay you back for everything you've done for me."

He grins and before he even opens his mouth, I know something sexual is coming. "You can pay me back in blowjobs."

"Derek!"

I shove him, but he just laughs and pulls me against him. "Okay, okay. Handjobs."

My ear rests on his chest, and I close my eyes. "It's a deal."

My leg won't stop shaking, and I can't stop looking at

the clock. It's almost one, so Derek should be home from work any time. For the first time since we met, I'm dreading seeing him.

When the front door opens, I jump up from the dining room table. My knees knock together.

Derek walks in and stops in his tracks. "What are you doing up? I thought you would have gone to sleep by now."

"I heard back from the prison," I say before I lose the nerve or my legs give out.

He shakes his head and takes a step back. "I told you I don't want you to do this."

"But I'm going to." I take a step closer, and my stomach tightens when he backs away. "Please don't make me go alone. Please say you'll be supportive."

He looks down. His fists are clenched at his side, and he won't stop shaking his head. "When?"

"February twelfth at ten o'clock in the morning."

He doesn't look up. "Where?"

"Chillicothe."

He nods and finally raises his head, but his jaw doesn't relax. It's tight but somehow he manages to say, "I won't make you go alone."

My shoulders relax. "Thank you. I've been terrified of telling you all day."

He leans against the doorframe. "I'm sorry. I don't want you to ever be afraid to tell me something."

"I wasn't afraid of you, silly. I was just worried that you wouldn't want to go with me. This is something I need to do, but I don't know if I can face it alone." The smile I give him shakes. "I *need* you Derek."

He takes a tiny step closer to me. I reach out to grab his hand and give it a squeeze.

"I need you too," he finally says.

He pulls me against him, and I rest my head on his chest. This is where I belong.

His hand makes lazy strokes up and down my spine.

"You parents aren't thrilled about this little arrangement we have going on here."

His hand doesn't stop moving, and with every stroke of his fingers, a tingle runs down my body. Maybe I should care what my parents think, or maybe I should just remind them I am technically an adult. "I know."

"It doesn't change your desire to be here?"

I lift my head so I can see him. "No. There isn't anywhere else I want to be right now."

The corner of his mouth turns up, and I squeeze my eyes shut when his lips brush against my forehead. "I don't want you to be anywhere else either."

I snuggle closer, savoring how safe he makes me feel. "We should get some sleep. We have to be in Columbus at ten tomorrow morning."

Derek doesn't say a word as he leads me to the bedroom.

Derek and I are about twenty minutes early to the coffee shop. He gets me my usual, but for once I don't drink it. My leg won't stop shaking as it is.

"You sure you don't want something it eat?" he asks.

My leg shakes, making the heel of my shoe tap against the floor. I can't seem to make it stop. "No. If I do I'm afraid I'm going to throw up."

He takes my hand. I'm glad he's here with me—if I had to face this alone I'd go nuts—but I'm still nervous as hell.

When Anne Rohr waltzes through the door, I know it's her. She looks exactly like the picture on the back of her book. Ten years haven't affected her at all. Her wavy brown hair is immaculate and her blue eyes sparkle when she scans the room. She's wearing a designer suit and heels that probably cost more than my entire wardrobe.

When our eyes meet, I stand, and she smiles. She flips her hair over her shoulders and strolls toward me, swaying her hips. I bet Stark just loves it when this woman comes to see him.

"Kara," she says, using the same breathless tone she did on the phone. She glances at her watch before taking my hand. "How nice to meet you."

"Dr. Rohr." My voice is scratchy, and I have to clear my throat.

"Anne, please." She gives me a sympathetic smile before motioning toward the table. "I have two hours."

"Th-thank you for seeing me." Why am I suddenly finding it difficult to breathe?

She presses her lips together. "I have to be honest. When I first got your call, I thought this was a joke. I wasn't even going to call you back."

"What convinced you?" Derek asks.

Anne's eyes snap toward him and then back to me. "Boyfriend?"

I'd forgotten he was there. "Yes. I'm sorry." My back is sweating. "This is Derek."

She gives him a tight smile then turns back to me. "I looked up your mom and did a little digging. Everything seemed to fit with what Jon has told me."

My throat tightens even more. "He's talked about my mom?"

"Only in general terms. He would never give her identity to me or anyone else—he said he wanted to protect her from any possible copycats." She narrows her eyes on my face. "He never mentioned you, though."

I swallow, but it doesn't help. "My mother never told him."

"I figured." She leans back and drums her fingers on the table. "You want to know who he is." It isn't a question, so I don't answer. "Your father—"

"Jonathon Stark. My father is Greg Jones." I'm trying to convince myself just as much as her.

"Of course. Jon is a textbook narcissistic sociopath. He's intelligent and well-educated, charming. Attractive.

On the surface, he's the exact kind of man you'd want to bring home to meet your parents. He was popular in school—even before going to Kent. "

I put my hand up to stop her. None of this is new. I want to know *who* my father is. "But he's crazy, right? Everything you're telling me is stuff I can get online or read in your book. I want to know who you think my father is. What about him made my mother fall in love? Why didn't he kill her?"

"I don't know the answer to those questions, but I can tell you what I think. Jon is the smartest man I've ever met. He's interesting to talk to and enjoyable to pass the time with. It's understandable why he was so loved by his students." Her voice is breathy, almost wistful, and her mouth turns up a little when she talks. Exactly the way my mom acted when she first started talking about him.

"You sound like you admire him."

"You can't understand how charming he is. He knows how to put you at ease, and there were times when I was talking to him about his childhood and his education that I would forget what a cold-blooded killer he was. I would even start to enjoy the time I spent with him."

"But you're a psychiatrist," Derek says. His lip curls up in disgust.

Anne doesn't even bat an eye. "But I'm still human. I'm not the only one that fell victim to him either. You can ask the detectives who were in charge of his case—I can give you their contact information if you want."

"Thanks." My insides are numb. Why is everyone so taken with this man? What if I go see him and I actually start to like him?

"But he was a killer," Derek says.

That snaps me out of it. No. I will *not* like this man. There's no way I can forget what he did, even if other people are able to.

Anne's brown hair bobs when she nods. "Oh yes. He's never denied that he killed those women. He confessed to the police after the mementos were found in his home. After his conviction he even bragged about the murders."

My stomach clenches and I squeeze Derek's leg under the table. "He's never expressed any remorse?"

Anne shakes her head. "People with antisocial personality disorder are incapable of feeling empathy for others. I don't believe that he can feel remorse. He's charming, but any emotions he shows are fake. They're copied. He's an expert at reading people and manipulating the situation. On top of that, he displays symptoms of narcissistic personality disorder, which has given him a sense of entitlement. He believes he deserves the praise of others—and somehow that confidence translates as charisma."

None of this coincides with how my mom talked about him. She really believes he loved her. Was she tricked? My grip on Derek's leg loosens, and I sit forward. "Are you saying that he *can't* feel?"

Anne frowns. "What do you mean?"

My question seemed pretty straightforward to me, but her eyes narrow on my face like I'm speaking a different language. "My mother really believes that he loved her. That's her only explanation for why he didn't kill her."

"I don't know what to say, Kara. When he talks about his relationship with your mom there is a certain amount of…dreaminess to his demeanor. He does seem *fond* of her, but it isn't any different than the way he sounds when he talks about his childhood bike. He has a strange attachment the bike he got for his birthday when he was twelve, and he often goes back to it when we talk. The two things seem to be the same in his mind. The bike and your mom are both just something he used to possess that give him a sense of pride."

Fond? You don't propose to someone you're *fond* of. Was he doing it for appearances? Maybe Anne's wrong. "So he didn't love her."

Anne's lips pull together into a tight line. "I'm sorry,

but I don't believe he's capable of love."

My entire body stiffens, and Derek wraps his hand around mine. "What made him this way?" he asks.

Anne glances at her watch. "We don't know exactly, but it's believed that a combination of genetics and environment can manifest itself as antisocial personality disorder."

"Genetics?" Until now I hadn't even considered inheriting something like this. My chest tightens, and I look at Derek. He uncoils his fingers and moves his arm to my shoulders.

Anne puts her hand up. "You don't need to worry, Kara. People are believed to have a genetic *predisposition* to something like this, but that doesn't necessarily mean that they'll turn into a serial killer or even have the urge. That's why we think environment plays a part in it as well—a trigger in early childhood. Something that would activate this gene. Like turning a light switch on so to speak. You were raised by loving parents and have maintained a normal life up to this point. If you were at all in danger of developing something like this there would have been clues by now. No matter how manipulative a person is, there are always clues." She smiles. "And the mere fact that you're worried about it is a big indicator that you are not in danger."

I still can't relax. Hearing details about this man has made the whole thing more real. The more Anne talks, the more the muscles in my arms ache from clenching my hands so tight. "So there *were* clues with Stark then? People suspected that there was something wrong with him?"

"His parents died before his arrest, so we don't know for sure, but it's believed that his father may have been scared of him from an early age. Jon had a good relationship with his mom for the most part—he even talks about her fondly. But he and his dad did not get along. Even though Stark didn't have a very violent past, there are stories about the two of them fighting. But his relationship with his mom deteriorated in his late teens, and I suspect that she may have been the first person that he actually killed."

My back goes rigid. That wasn't in her book. "I didn't read that anywhere."

"It's part of the reason I'm still visiting him. There are parts of his early years that he still refuses to talk about, and I'm hoping to get him to open up since the end is so near. His mother had a heart condition and died in her sleep, and it was written off as a heart attack. But there's always been something about it that bothered me. I personally believe that Stark smothered her in her sleep."

Anne's face suddenly goes out of focus. I blink, and it comes back.

"The family didn't get an autopsy?" Derek asks.

Anne glances at her watch again. She must be a busy woman. "There was no reason. She was older when she had Stark, so she was well into her sixties by then and her heart condition had been an issue for a while. She'd even suffered a heart attack a few years earlier."

"What makes you think he did that?" My leg has started to shake. Do I really want to know the answer to this? Do I want to learn about his childhood? The lack of information about his early years bothered me before, but now I'm not so sure.

"Something he said to me once about his mother turning on him when he was sixteen. Stark claims that his father had always been quick to think the worst of him, but that his mother doted on him. She'd always defended her son, but shortly after he turned sixteen things changed. He won't admit to anything specific, but there was a time in his early teens when a large number of pets in his neighborhood went missing. I personally believe he was responsible for that, and that his mother either suspected or found out. There must have been some kind of confrontation that resulted in him killing her."

My stomach lurches and I lean forward. "I think I'm

going to be sick."

Derek rubs my back. My face heats up and he whispers in my ear, but his warm breath only makes it worse. The noises around me become dull and far away, like someone is turning the volume down in the room. My mouth fills with repulsive-tasting saliva. Derek fans my face, and I close my eyes.

"Are you going to pass out?" Derek's voice echoes in my ears like he's in a tunnel.

"I don't know. Probably."

"Scoot her chair back." Anne is in the tunnel with Derek. "Kara, put your head between your legs."

Her words don't make a lot of sense. My head is jerked back and my chair screeches across the floor; it's louder than a freight train. Someone shoves my head down and tells me to breathe, and I focus on moving air in and out of my lungs. In. Out. In. Out. My head is heavy, like it's made of lead.

Slowly, I start to cool off and the noises get louder. Derek keeps rubbing my back. "Are you feeling better?" His face is right next to my ear.

I swallow. My mouth still tastes like crap. "Yes."

The room sways a little when I start to sit up, and immediately a second set of hands are on my shoulder. "Easy," Anne says.

My cheeks are still warm, but at least my head doesn't feel like it weighs a thousand pounds anymore.

"You okay now?" Derek's brown eyes swim in a sea of worry. He has lines on his forehead I've never seen before, and absentmindedly I trace my finger across them. He's too cute and sweet to have to worry about me like this. I'm a mess. He deserves someone whose life is less complicated.

But if he leaves me, I'm pretty sure I'll die, so I say, "I'm okay."

"When's the last time you ate something?" Anne is still standing in front of me with her arms crossed over her chest. She doesn't look worried, just authoritative. "You're pale and shaky."

"I don't know."

Derek swears and gets to his feet. "I should have made you eat. I'm getting you something."

He starts to walk away, but Anne grabs his arm. "Get her some juice to drink too."

I hate juice.

When Derek's gone, Anne sits back down. "I'm sorry. I know this is a lot to take in."

"A few weeks ago I didn't even know Jonathon Stark existed." I close my eyes and count to ten before opening them again. "I want to know more. What else do you know about his childhood?"

"Are you sure you can handle it?"

"No, but I need to know what I'm in for."

"What do you mean?"

"I want to know who this man is before I meet him."

She slowly shakes her head. "No, Kara. I didn't know you were thinking about going to see him. I thought you were talking to me so you didn't have to meet him. Don't do this."

She's against me too? I would have thought she'd be in favor of it. Isn't she still seeing him after all these years? "No one understands, but I have to know who this man is."

Anne keeps shaking her head. I wish she'd stop; it's making my temples pound. "He's scheduled to be executed in three months. Let him die believing that he isn't leaving anything behind. You don't understand. He believes he's some kind of god or maybe even something bigger."

Bigger than God? She wasn't joking when she said he was narcissistic. I don't see what it has to do with me though. "What can it hurt to go visit him?"

Anne grinds her teeth. "He'll see you as a way for him to live on. Don't give him that satisfaction."

Anne's face is out of focus again, but this time it isn't because I'm close to passing out. I swipe my hand across my eyes and cringe when I pull my arm back. It's smeared with black. Damn mascara. Why am I crying anyway?

Anne pulls her purse open and whips out a tissue. "Kara, I get your desire to meet him, but there has to be another way. Trust me when I say that meeting him would be a mistake."

"Where else am I going to get answers to my questions?"

She presses her lips together for a second and looks over my head. When her blue eyes meet mine she sighs. "Your uncle may be able to answer a few questions."

"Stark's brother? I didn't think anyone knew where he was."

Anne grinds her teeth again and glances back at her watch. "I have to go soon." She drums her fingernails on the table. "I don't know where he is, but I have a way of contacting him. I can get him a message, let him know about you and leave it up to him to make the next move. There's no guarantee that he'll contact you, but it's worth a shot. When were you planning on going to see Stark?"

"I have an appointment on February twelfth."

"I'll send him an e-mail right away."

Anne stands when Derek comes back with two juices boxes and two blueberry muffins. "I have to leave. Please think about what I said, Kara. If you have any more questions call or e-mail me." She pulls a card out of her purse and hands it to me. "This is my direct number. I sincerely hope you change your mind about meeting Stark."

Derek tenses, but I don't look at him. I already know he doesn't approve.

"I'll think about it, but I doubt I'll change my mind."

"We'll talk again then," Anne says.

"I'm sure I'll have a lot of questions afterward."

CHAPTER TWENTY-THREE

My hand shakes as I sign into the prison log.

"You're going to be alright," Derek says.

The woman behind the desk frowns at him. "You weren't on the list of visitors."

"I'm going in alone." Just saying it makes my stomach lurch.

She pushes her glasses up with her middle finger. "You're going to need to surrender your purse in the next room. There will also be a metal detector and pat-down to make sure you're not carrying any concealed weapons. Please have a seat in the waiting area until you are called." She jerks the clipboard out of my hand and points to a few couches.

Thankfully, Derek holds my hand when we head across the room. My legs are wobbly and if he wasn't here I'd fall for sure. How am I going to make it through those doors without him?

We take a seat next to a woman in her twenties. She has a baby balanced on her knee, and she smiles when our eyes meet. The sight makes me want to throw up, so I have to look away. At least my mom wasn't brainwashed by Stark. That baby could have been me. Growing up visiting my insane father in prison. I guess there are things to be thankful for.

"You can still change your mind," Derek says.

"I can't." I swallow and work on keeping my voice steady. "I have to do this."

He frowns, but he doesn't let go of my hand. We've barely spoken today. He isn't angry, just stressed, and I'm too terrified to think of anything to say. I can't wait until this is over.

A black man in a suit walks into the lobby and scans the room. His eyes rest on me briefly before he walks to the receptionist. They whisper for a few seconds, and then she points in my direction. My stomach turns inside out. Is it time already? I expected a guard to come get me.

Derek's hand tightens around mine when the man heads our way. He stops in front of us and wipes his bald head; he's sweating even though it's February and can't be more than thirty degrees outside.

His eyes move over my face for a few seconds, and then he clears his throat. "Ms. Jones?"

I nod and get to my feet, and Derek jumps up with me. "Y-yes." *Hold it together, Kara.* I take a deep breath and try again. "I'm Kara Jones." Better.

"My name is Doug Wilson, and I'm the warden here. Would you mind stepping into my office for a few minutes so we can have a little chat?"

This is strange. But maybe they do this with all first-time visitors? Seems like the warden would have more important things to do, but I can't figure out why else he'd want to talk to me.

"Of course." I try to sound confident.

Derek squeezes my hand. Right, Derek. How could I have forgotten he's here when he's holding my hand? "If you don't mind, my boyfriend is going to come with me."

The warden tilts his head to the side and studies Derek, and then his eyes move down to our entwined hands. The hair on the back of my neck stands up, and my scalp tingles.

"I suppose that would be okay." He doesn't sound very sure of himself.

He leads us through the door he just came out of and down a silent hall. The warden's shoes click on the green and white linoleum and echo through the hall. There isn't another sound anywhere other than the pounding of my heart.

He stops at the end of the hall and motions for us to follow him through an open door. It's an office with a large wooden desk in the center and two chairs in front of it. He points to the chairs and shuts the door behind him.

"Please have a seat," he says, crossing to the other side of the desk.

His chair is almost as tall as he is and covered in dark leather. It swivels slightly when he lowers himself into it. Derek and I take the other seats, and I never let go of his hand. Right now, I'm squeezing it so hard the bones in his fingers have to be grinding together, but he doesn't complain. The warden frowns and lays his hands on top of the desk, pressing his fingertips together like some kind of mad scientist working on an evil scheme. It doesn't help me calm down.

"You meet with everyone that comes to visit an inmate?" Derek asks, breaking the silence.

The warden shakes his head. "No, I don't." He turns his eyes to me. "I have to say, I almost denied your request for a visit. Curiosity won out though. It isn't often that we get a request from someone claiming to be the child of a serial killer. And so close to his execution date. It raised quite a few red flags."

My mouth drops open, and Derek blows out through his teeth. It never occurred to me how strange my request would look, but I guess it should have. Stark has been in here for eighteen years. A daughter popping up just a few months before he's scheduled to be put to death does seem suspicious. Of course, I'm not sure what they suspect me of. Trying to break him out? Do I look crazy?

"So," the warden says, sitting forward. He lays his hands flat on the top of the desk, and I'm glad; the evil scientist thing was making me squirm. "Why don't you tell me what you're doing here so I can decide whether or not to let you see Stark?"

"What do you mean?"

Derek shakes his head. "Exactly what are you accusing her of?"

"Don't treat me like a fool, because I'm not. I've worked in the prison system my entire adult life, and I've been the warden here for fifteen years. We get all kind of crazies in here. Fans, wannabes, women that have been seduced by Stark. So which is it, Ms. Jones? Which one are you?"

"Wait!" I drop Derek's hand and rub my forehead. "Seduced? How is he able to even talk to these people?"

The warden glances toward the clock. "Pen pals. The mail is monitored, but Stark is smart. I wouldn't put anything past him."

I massage my temples and stare at the desk. What have I gotten myself into? How crazy is this guy? I can still back down, but we've come so far. To leave now just seems stupid.

"I really am his daughter." The warden snorts, so I raise my head and meet his eyes. "I'm serious."

The warden leans back and listens without interruption as I go through the whole story. It stings. This is the first time I've told a stranger about my mom's affair without a shitload of alcohol in me, and admitting Stark is my father is probably the hardest thing I've ever done. Especially to this man who seems to know exactly what kind of sociopath he's dealing with.

"So you met with Anne Rohr?" The warden says when I've finished. I nod, and he shakes his head. "Didn't she warn you not to come? She should have told you."

"She told me."

He stands up. "You should have listened. Stark has two

months left. His clemency hearing is in three weeks and there's no way in hell the governor is going to let him weasel his way out of this. He's out of appeals and his time has run out. Everything so far has been a green light. You should have just let him go. Now." He runs his hand across his bald scalp. "Well I don't know what this is going to do to him, but I can guarantee that he's going to do everything in his power to put this execution off."

Derek and I stand as well, and my head pounds. It's hard to really focus on what he's saying. "What do you mean? You just said his time is up."

The warden's lips pull down even more. "He's a smart son of a bitch. If there's a way out, he'll find it, and I don't doubt that he has a few tricks up his sleeve still. You'll see."

Why does everyone act like this when they talk about Stark? Like he's some kind of manipulative guru? He can't possibly be smart enough to figure out a way to postpone his execution again. Can he?

"Are you going to let me see him?"

"Other than the fact that I think this is a truly bad idea, I don't have any real reason to keep you out." He motions toward the door. "So yeah, I'm going to let you see him."

The second the door shuts I start to shake.

"Last booth," the guard behind me says.

His deep voice booms through the room and I let out a little yelp, but I don't look back. I walk toward the last chair. There are dividers that separate the visiting areas, but at the moment I'm the only visitor here. I stop in front of the glass that will separate me and Stark and grip the back of the chair. Unlike the movies, there's no phone. There's actually a small slot at the bottom. The guards explained to me that it's there so the prisoner can hold hands with his visitors. Thankfully, Stark will be shackled.

If he touches me, I'm pretty sure I'll have to spend the rest of my life in an insane asylum.

I take the seat and pull nervously at the hem of my shirt. They took my cell phone and purse, so I don't have anything to fool with to keep my hands busy, which means I end up drumming my fingernails on the counter. It echoes through the room and makes my heart beat even faster.

A door clicks on the other side of the glass, and my fingers stop moving. There's shuffling and low voices, the sound of metal clinking. Every noise causes my anxiety level to go up a few notches.

When Stark comes into view, I get to my feet. I can't help it. He's wearing orange prison clothes, and his hands are cuffed in front of him. A chain stretches from the cuffs down to the floor where I can only assume his ankles are shackled as well. A guard walks on each side of him, sticking to him like glue until he sinks into the chair. The guards step back, but don't go too far.

And then I'm face-to-face with Jonathon Stark.

I don't make a move to sit down, and he doesn't speak. For what seems like hours we stare at each other. His soft brown eyes take in every move I make, every breath I suck in. Mine are just as eager to study him. Even after all these years in prison he's still good-looking. His dark-brown hair is graying slightly, but just around the temples—it looks distinguished—and his face is almost completely unlined. Other than the prison cuffs and clothes, he looks normal.

"You look exactly like Charlotte," he finally says.

My legs give out, and I collapse into the chair. It almost tips over, but I manage to catch myself on the wall. The chair legs bang against the floor so hard the sound vibrates through the room. One of the guards takes a step forward, but he doesn't say anything.

"H-how did you know?"

"I told you." His voice is smooth and emotionless. His lips twitch and turn up into a smile that makes goose bumps pop up on every inch of my skin. "What I want to know is, why Charlotte Meyer's daughter would come visit me."

This isn't what I expected, and for a few seconds my mouth is so dry that I can't form any words. "I-I came." I swallow. "I came because I wanted to meet my father before he died."

A slow smile spreads across Stark's face and he sits back. "Well this is a surprise."

He doesn't say anything else, and his calm demeanor puts my nerves on edge—the edge of a cliff. I grip the counter, and I try to remember everything I wanted to ask him. But my mind is completely blank. If only they had let me bring my notebook.

"What's wrong?" Stark is still smiling. Even though I know it isn't real, it looks so genuine a part of me is drawn in by it. "Do I disappoint? You'll have to excuse the clothes. Orange has never been my color."

"Did you love my mom?" I blurt out.

"Charlotte, Charlotte. What fun she was!" He purses his lips, and my stomach flips. I do have his mouth. "Love? Not exactly. I did enjoy having her around. She was the only woman I was ever with that I didn't want to strangle." He laughs and lifts his hands, but the chains stop him from bringing them higher than his chest. "Just a figure of speech!"

Except it's not. The blood flowing through my veins turns to ice. If I didn't have so much I needed to know I'd run out of here, probably screaming. But I have to know who this man is.

I plant my feet firmly on the ground and lean forward. "So you didn't love her, but you did propose to her. Why? I want to know what you wanted out of a relationship with my mom."

His smile widens. How does he manage to look so relaxed with his hands in shackles? It can't be comfortable. "You have her spirit."

Spirit? Is he joking again? My mom hasn't shown an ounce of spirit in my entire life, at least none that I've seen.

Stark inhales. "I enjoyed your mother's company."

"Were you going to kill her like the others?"

"So that's it. You came to find out what saved her."

"And to find out who you are. What your family was like. Your childhood."

"What made me like this." The *S* hisses through his teeth, making him sound like a snake. He is a snake. I can see it now, what everyone was talking about.

"Are you going to tell me?"

He sits back like he's lounging by a pool with a margarita in his hand. "You first."

I blink and shake my head. "What do you mean?"

"Tell me about you. Your life, your mom. I'm guessing by your last name that she married that buffoon she was dating before me. Greg, was it? I met him a few times. He was weak."

"Don't talk about my dad like that."

"But my dear girl, *I* am your father." He flashes his teeth. I grip the counter tighter. The smile is so sinister I expect his teeth to be pointed, but they're as straight and white as teeth in a toothpaste commercial.

"No, you're not."

"Doesn't matter, genetics don't lie."

I hate that he's right. No matter how much I want Greg Jones to be my dad, there will always be a part of Stark flowing through my veins. It makes my stomach churn, but I fight to maintain control.

"What do you want to know?" I ask.

"Are you going to college?"

I fight to keep my body from shaking. "I was, and I will go back. There was an accident and then all this happened." I gesture toward him and despite my best efforts, my hands tremble.

"Ah…so you just found out about me. Explains why

you waited so long to visit." He shifts, and the metal chains clang against the chair. "What are you studying?"

"Undeclared."

"Boyfriend?"

I grip my jeans. "Yes."

"And your mother is well?"

My mouth won't open, so I just nod. Why is he so interested in all of this? Why does he care about my mom? I just want to get my questions out there and move on. Sitting this close to him is turning my body into a ball of tension.

"Now my turn." The words come out with so much force, I'm surprised the room doesn't shake.

Stark sighs like this is the most tedious thing he's ever been through. "Ah…the childhood. Why is everyone so interested in where I came from? I had a mom and dad just like everyone, and just like everyone they died." He raises his hands again, and the chains jingle. "Although I suppose you of all people deserve to hear some of the details. You are part of me after all."

My stomach lurches and Stark smiles. Is he taking enjoyment in my torture? What am I thinking? Of course he is. That's why he's in here.

"I want to know about my grandparents, my uncle."

"Why don't you ask what you really want to know? Did they beat me? Starve me? Did they teach me to be a killer? The answers are all no. They did none of those things. My mother was sweet. She loved me despite my flaws." He makes a sweeping motion with his hands, but once again the shackles stop him from raising them too high. "But my father was strict and controlling."

"Dr. Rohr said the two of you didn't get along."

His eyebrows shoot up. "You met Anne? How lovely. It's been a few months since she came to visit, but I suppose she'll make time to get here now. With the execution so close and you showing up, this will give her all kinds of fun questions to ask me."

"What made you like this?"

"Haven't you heard," he says, leaning closer. "I was born this way."

Stark laughs and I scoot my chair further away. He's too close. The glass is too thin and the slot is too big. I want out of here. Maybe I shouldn't have come.

But no. There is still one thing I need to ask him. "Were you going to kill my mom?"

Stark leans back again and his smile morphs into something threatening. "Was I going to kill her? You know, they've been trying to drag your mother's name out of me for the past nineteen years. Anne in particular has been very interested in her. Charlotte is the only relationship I ever had that didn't end...poorly."

My stomach twists. Does that mean there are other victims? Surely he dated women when he was younger? Is that why Anne keeps coming?

"So you killed before Kent?" The question pops out before I can stop it, and immediately I regret asking.

"How very perceptive of you." For the first time Stark takes his eyes off my face. He looks down at his hands. "That's the theory anyway." He looks back up. "I like to keep people guessing."

I want out of here. "My mom. I want to know about my mom."

"I was drawn to your mother the second I met her. She had life in her. The same spirit that all my victims had. That you have."

Bile rises in my throat, and I swallow it down. I can't get sick in here. "Go on."

"But unlike my other victims, she was immune to my charms." His smile widens, and if I didn't know he was a psychopath, I'd think it was the most charming smile I'd ever seen. "Almost immune. It took a lot of time to seduce her, something that I wasn't used to."

"Why not just kidnap her?"

"The seduction was part of the game for me. It made

the end so much more…satisfying."

I scoot my chair back a few more inches. "So you were going to kill her."

"That was my original plan, but it took so long to get her…things changed." His eyes never waver from my face. "She was a challenge to get. It made me want to keep her around."

My chest is tight. She came so close. If she'd been like all those other women and thrown herself at him, things would have turned out so differently. I wouldn't be here. It's almost too much to take.

I have my answers and I'm more than ready to leave, but I can't make my legs work enough to stand up. Stark watches me, but I can't read the expression on his face. Amusement maybe?

After a few seconds, he leans even closer to the glass. As close as he can get without pressing his nose up against it. "I have to tell you, this has been a very pleasant surprise. All these years sitting here in this hole and my biggest regret has been that I had no one to pass on my legacy to. And here you come, waltzing in at the eleventh hour like a hero."

My chest gets tighter and I gasp for air. I'm back in that car, with the steering wheel pressed against me. All I can get into my lungs are teaspoonful's of air. Not enough to keep me from gasping, not enough to get words out. Barely enough to keep me alive.

"Please say that you'll come to see me again. It has been so nice to meet you."

I manage to suck in just enough air to say, "You'll be dead soon, so it won't matter."

"Don't count me out yet," Stark says. "I have a whole arsenal at my disposal, and I haven't even exhausted half of my ammo yet."

Oh my God, Anne was right. I get to my feet, and the chair falls over. My legs are barely supporting me when I stumble toward the door, but thankfully, the guard meets me halfway. Stark says something behind me, but I can't focus. My heart pounds so hard it vibrates in my ears, and all my energy is going toward making my legs move so I can get away.

If I can go, the rest of my life and never see Stark again I will die happy.

When I reach the lobby, I practically fall into Derek's arms. The second they're around me, the tears I've been trying to hold back spill over. He leads me to the couch, rubbing my head and whispering soothing words, but I can't stop sobbing.

"What happened?" he asks.

"I-I can't." My words are hiccups. I sniff and inhale, swallowing as many of the sobs as I can, so I can get the words out. "I can't talk about it right now."

"I'm sorry." Derek holds me tighter.

"Take me home. I want to see my dad."

Derek doesn't let go of my hand until he puts the car in park. My dad's car is in the driveway even though it's the middle of the day. He said he was going to take a few weeks' vacation, so I shouldn't be surprised.

"Are you alright?" Derek asks for the hundredth time.

"I'm okay. Now." I shake my head because I still can't talk about it. Maybe I'll never be able to really talk about it. "Seeing him with my own eyes was…" I can't come up with the words to describe it, and when I look at Derek he frowns. "This is what you were worried about, wasn't it?"

"I just didn't know if you were strong enough to deal with it all."

"I get it. But I had to know."

"Are you going to tell your parents that you went to see him? I should know before we go in."

"Maybe my dad. I'm not sure my mom could handle it. You know, Stark made a few comments about how much spirit she had, but she's always been so weak. That must be because of him."

Derek runs his hand through his hair. "Can you blame her?"

"No, I can't. In fact, now that I've met Stark I'm not really sure if I can blame her for anything. As much as I hate to admit it, I understand why she lied to me now."

"So you forgive her?"

"I'm going to try." I reach for the door handle. "But first I'm going inside so I can see my dad. My real dad."

Mom and Dad are in the kitchen. Laughing. It should be comforting, but it makes my stomach clench to hear that twinkling sound come out of my mom's mouth. Understanding and forgiving are two different things—it's going to take some time.

They freeze when we walk in. My dad smiles and comes over to give me a hug, but mom stays where she is. I throw myself in his arms and squeeze him so tight he pretends gasp for air. It makes me laugh and brings tears to my eyes at the same time.

"Careful there, Kara, I'm not as young as I used to be," he whispers against my head, but he squeezes me back.

When I pull away he frowns. "Why the tears?"

I sniff. "They're tears of joy. I'm just glad to see you, that's all."

He cocks his head to the side and his eyes go to Derek, but he nods. "Well I'm glad to see you too."

"Are you staying for dinner?" Mom asks. She hasn't moved from her original position, but there's a hesitant smile on her lips.

"Yeah."

My voice is thick and both my parents narrow their eyes on me. It feels familiar and oddly comforting. The problem with being an only child—your parents' world revolves around you.

I take a hesitant step toward my mom, and her eyes widen. "Do you need help with dinner?"

Her blue eyes, so like my own, fill with tears. "I would love help, Kara."

When I walk by Dad, he squeezes my hand, and my eyes meet Derek's. He smiles, and his super-Zoloft powers seep inside my body. Or maybe that isn't it. Maybe it's about being here in my house with my parents, and really realizing for the first time how lucky I am. My mom lied to me, but things could have been so much worse. She could have been one of Stark's victims, or she could have been so brainwashed by him, she stuck by him all these years. She chose to lie, and right or wrong, it was the best choice for our family.

EPILOGUE

It's dark when I step outside. Man, it's going to suck working in a building with no windows, but at least I found a job. It's only my second day, but it isn't bad. I could be working in fast food.

"See you tomorrow, Kara," Sophia says with a wave.

One of my new coworkers—and a chance to actually make some friends who live in the area. That would be nice. Especially since Derek has been working hard on trying to talk me into staying in Dayton. I haven't told him yet, but it's worked. There's no way I could leave him now; he's like a drug.

"Good night," I call, turning my cell phone on as I head for my car. Derek's car, really.

One missed call and one text from Derek. Seeing his name still sends a shiver down my spine. I'm not sure if I'll ever get enough of him.

Derek: *Come over to the bar when you get off work. I miss you!*

Like he could keep me away.

Kara: *B there. Just don't let Gray Beard make me walk the plank!*

I pull up my voicemail and unlock the car. It plays in my ear as I duck inside. It's from Anne. I shouldn't be surprised; it's March fifth. Today was Stark's clemency hearing.

"Kara, it's Anne. Listen, um…" She pauses. "Shit. Just give me a call when you get this. No matter how late it is. There's been a development."

It cuts off. A development? What does that mean?

There's no way Stark was granted clemency. No way.

My hands shake when I push the button to call Anne back, and each second it rings without her answering makes my heart beat harder. But when she finally picks up, everything in my body freezes.

"Kara. I've been waiting for your call." She sounds even more breathless than usual.

"I was at work." The temperature in the car shoots up about twenty degrees, and my palms start to sweat. I wipe them on my jeans.

Anne takes a deep breath, and my throat goes dry. "Stark was granted a stay of execution."

I squeeze my eyes shut. There's no way I heard her right.

But I know I did.

"What does that mean? A life sentence?"

"No. He'll still be put to death, but his execution has been delayed."

I can't think, can't breathe. For the first time since I went to see Stark my chest is tight, and I feel like I'm being crushed by that steering wheel all over again. "Why? How could this happen?"

"There are more victims, Kara."

All the air leaves my lungs. "What?"

"We've always suspected that Stark started killing earlier. I told you that. He's finally admitted to it and agreed to reveal who his earlier victims are. The governor had to agree. The families of these women deserve to know what happened."

I massage my head, but it's still pounding. "I know." And I do know, but that doesn't mean I have to like it.

"There's more."

My stomach clenches and I know what's coming. I squeeze my eyes shut like that will stop Anne from saying it, stop Stark from being my father, stop him from being crazy. Stop me from remembering.

"He wants to see you."

"Why?" I croak.

"I told you this would happen, Kara."

"I don't need to hear I told you so right now, Anne," I snap. "What does he want with me?"

"He wants to get to know his daughter."

"Or he won't reveal anything."

"This is how Stark works." She sounds so callous. If she were here, I'd punch her in the face.

Get to know me? More like torture me. Is he going to use me to confess his crimes? Relay the grisly details of his murder spree to the police using me as a medium? I won't do that.

"I don't want to hear any of the details," I say, shaking my head. She can't see me, so I know it's a waste, but I can't sit still any longer. My body starts to shake.

"That's not what he wants. He doesn't want to confess to you, just to get to know you." She pauses. "And he wants to meet your boyfriend."

My eyes snap open. Derek? I can't drag him into this, not this far. He's been through so much already.

"Why?" I whisper.

"I don't know what he's after, but he made a big deal about a father's duty. He's a narcissist. Maybe he really thinks his approval will mean something to you, or maybe he just wants to torture you."

My eyes squeeze shut when my stomach turns inside out. That pizza for lunch was a bad idea. "Don't try to sugar coat it or anything."

"You should know by now that isn't my way." She's silent for a second, and when I don't speak she finally says, "Will you do it?"

I let out a bitter laugh and lay my forehead on the

steering wheel. "Do I have a choice?"

"We always have choices."

No we don't. Not when it comes to the really big things in life. "I can't talk about this right now. Let me call you later."

"I need to let the FBI know," Anne says. "They want to get moving on this, Kara. Some of these murders are close to thirty years old."

Thirty years. How horrible to go that long without knowing what happened to your loved one. Much as I hate to admit it, I have to do whatever it takes to help. Letting the family of Stark's victims suffer would be selfish.

But I still can't talk about it now. "Just tell them to call me."

I hang up and lean back against the headrest.

He can't hurt me. Not for real. No matter how manipulative he is, he's still just a man. And I have the advantage because I know he's insane.

But what about Derek? Do I take him with me? And my parents? They still have no idea I went to see Stark the first time. There's no way I'll be able to hide it from them now. What will this do to them? To my mom! They're working on things, going to counseling…getting back to normal. If there is such a thing.

But I can't focus on all of that right now. I can't let Stark rule every minute of my life. Derek is what I need. I start the car and take a deep breath. No matter what happens, I know Derek will be by my side. Even Stark can't destroy that.

ABOUT THE AUTHOR

Kate L. Mary is a stay-at-home mother of four and an Air Force wife. She spent most of her life in a small town just north of Dayton, Ohio where she and her husband met at the age of twelve. Since their marriage in 2002, they have lived in Georgia, Mississippi, South Carolina, and California.

Kate's love of books and writing has helped her survive countless husbandless nights. She enjoys any post-apocalyptic story – especially if zombies are involved – as long as there is a romantic twist to give the story hope. Kate prefers nerdy, non-traditional heroes that can make you laugh to hunky pieces of man-meat, and her love of wine and chocolate is legendary among her friends and family. She currently resides in Oklahoma with her husband and children.

You can visit her website at www.KateLMary.com

31320069R00134

Made in the USA
Charleston, SC
13 July 2014